Lesser Evils: Ten Quartets

Gary Soto

Arte Publico Press
Houston

Acknowledgements

These essays have appeared in *Another Chicago Magazine*, *Puerto del Sol*, *Yellow Silk* and *ZYZZYVA*.
Lesser Evils was written from August to October 1986.

This book is made possible through a grant from the National Endowment for the Arts, a federal agency.

Arte Publico Press
University of Houston
Houston, Texas 77004

Soto, Gary.
    Lesser evils: ten quartets / Gary Soto.
    p.   cm.
    ISBN 0-934770-77-8
    1. Soto, Gary—Biography. 2. Poets,
American—20th century—Biography. 1. Title.
PS3569.072Z468   1987
814.54—dc19   87-20901
                                                 CIP

Contents

Between Points

I can't get over how some are dying while others are being born. At the cemetery in Colma ladders lean against stone fences. Why are they there? Do the dead need ladders to get where they are going, or just blackness and the heavy smell of wet earth? And I've seen the other end of death, a child being born, the clots of blood, the startled eyes, the wild crying. The nurse cleared fluid from the newborn's throat, tapped a knee, weighed her. The child only cried harder when she was brought to her mother's arms.

I'm between these two points, the first days and the last days, and I'm wondering what I should do about this. Earlier in the day I went to a conference on minorities as represented in the media, was in fact a speaker. When it came to my turn, I was amazed how my mouth began to move, and move well because people were shaking their heads in agreement and laughing when it was time to laugh. But I only half-believed my words and hardly believed anyone else, especially when it was proposed that we initiate a nationwide boycott against Hollywood. I'm for this, a boycott, and even opened the same mouth that only minutes before was perfectly articulate and said, "Yeah, let's do a boycott." But I also think it's absurd, unworkable, and naive. Hollywood would suck on cigars and blow smoke at us. They make millions from the often not-too-bright movie goers. If we had shook everyone down for money at that conference, we might have gotten two, maybe three (before lunch that is), hundred dollars. With such a bankroll, how could we ever bring Hollywood down to its knees?

I suppose we get to a point when we think no one knows anything. These last days my wife and daughter have been out of town. I've been eating sandwiches for dinner, tuna last night and tuna again tonight, with chips and pickles and glasses of beer. The first evening I sat with my meager plate and watched the news. There was a story of a family whose relatives had died by a terrorist attack, yet another clip of the shuttle Explorer blowing up, thirty seconds for Chernobyl, a few glimpses of our politicians, two of whom were under indictment for pocketing campaign contributions. I ate my sandwiches and felt sick.

When I was young I thought I could help. I joined college groups, protested, bought very little, used a bike instead of a car, and lived like a monk in an unfurnished apartment: there was my sleeping bag, my typewriter, and fruit on the counter. My friends were like me, poor sparrows hopping on a dry lawn, and my girlfriend, only daughter of Japanese poor folk, was a good reason to make things simple. I was in love, crazy, rode a bike to get where I was going, and bought nothing on the open market.

When I was young I thought I could help. Now I'm not so sure. Rain forests are being slashed at ten acres an hour in Brazil, and because they're three time zones away, on another continent, I continue eating my sandwiches and assume I'm not involved. And anyway, I tell myself, just what could I do? What politician could I grab by the throat and beg that he do something?

And my family, wife and daughter and cat with triangle shaped head, are happy. And so are my nephews, my sister, my 'little brother,' white kid living in the Projects who'll pull out in time and make it on his own. They're hopeful, busy in

8

their lives, and believe in nothing that I say.

Today I don't feel good about being where I am, aged thirty-four, and a bright childhood gone and the mad-gray years ahead of me. The earth knows how to dismantle flesh bone by bone and keep us in the ground. The sea is no help: it will wash the dead over and over without rest, if by chance we should die by water. The ones I love dearly will die, and our end, east or west, is a stone that won't roll back.

The Girl on the Can of Peas

My first love? I was five and sitting in our dirt yard on Braly Street. My brother Rick was hanging by almighty luck in the almond tree and making bomb sounds. He flicked unripe almonds at me, calling me names, but I didn't turn around or get mad because I was mesmerized by the girl on the can of peas, which I had pulled out of the garbage. I had also taken out a milk carton, a soup can, a tuna can, and was assembling them into a city that I intended to burn with matches.

The girl possessed a flushed face, blond curls, a dance of light in her eyes, which were looking right at me and which had me feeling embarrassed because I had spikey hair and sticky peach stains at the corners of my mouth. I peeled the label off the can and ran up the brick steps into the house to hide it, and in my room I stared at her with a longing that was new to me. But in time I returned outside, worn out from the deep feelings I had shared with her, and played soldiers with Rick. Later we wandered into the alley to look for fruit—plums and peaches—and found both in the yard of a Japanese family, whose grandpa chased us with a rake all the way to the railroad tracks at Van Ness Avenue. But he stopped there and just swore. We walked up onto the tracks where we set rocks on the oily rails and waited to see what would happen when a train passed. When one did arrive in the distance, slow as a cloud, we hid behind a telephone pole, no doubt visible to everyone, feeling giddy that a train wreck was going to take place in our young lives. We held our breath as its black shadow approached and the engine roared in our chests. But not much happened. Sparks flowered and snapped when the wheels struck the rocks, which were kicked away and at once mingled with other rocks.

On the way home we sneaked past the Japanese yard where we heard the chatter of mad voices. In the kitchen we heated tortillas, smeared them with a knife blade of butter, and rolled them into fat flutes. We took them to our bedroom, which was a converted sun porch, and ate them. A vein of melted butter ran down my forearm to my elbow but I didn't care. I was happy, so happy that I showed Rick the label of the girl on the can of peas. He held it in his small hands like a treasure map and together we went dreamy with her beauty.

Rick asked where I had found it. I pointed to the alley and said a garbage can. Rick's face brightened up. "I know where she lives," he said. I looked at him dumbfounded because I couldn't imagine that someone so delicate and rich would live near a poor street like ours. He told me she lived only two or three blocks away. Together we went outside, up the alley like a couple of quiet cats, past the broom factory and the *whamwham* of its machinery, to the street our mother warned us never to cross. "She lives over there," Rick pointed. I looked and saw only a line of diesel trucks, vacant lots, brick buildings humming with work, but no houses where she might live.

"No sir," I said with a screwed-up face, being no one's fool.

"Not there, stupid!" he snapped, "three streets from there. That's where the rich got their houses. They got the trucks parked there 'cause they don't want to see us."

It sounded plausible to me, but still I was scared of mother and her warning never to cross the street. I stood on

11

the curb, my arms limp as wings, wanting to cross because the street didn't seem that scary. I could run over there, I thought, and be back in a flash. I bit my lip and begged Rick to come along. When he shook his head no, I stepped hesitantly from the curb, looking both ways, and then scurried like a rabbit across the street. I was breathless. I looked back at Rick who, with cupped hands, was yelling that I was a dead boy on the floor when mother found out. "He's a stupid queer Mexican," I said to myself, scared and almost crying as I watched Rick disappear up the alley on the way home where he would wait on the front porch for mother to return from Redi-Spud.

I walked past those diesels only to find another yard of diesels, and rusty buildings, a tire company. After a while I was so lost and confused at not finding the girl on the can of peas that I just sat down and cried into my arms.

How did I get back? I don't know, except I remember later that spring my cat Boots crossed that street, black asphalt snake of misfortune, and returned home with a sliver of wood in her eye. She died the next day, but her face, twisted with pain, stayed in my memory for years, long after I had lost that label of the girl on the can of peas.

Schemes

Coins like rain, dollar bills, pockets thick with IOUs, the mailbox fat with envelopes that smell of checks. It's morning and my wife, asleep next to me, is oblivious to my greed, which is wet as a wide yawn. Money. This is what I want, big money, signed-over checks, and even the icy cold quarter my finger licks up as I go from pay phone to pay phone.

Greed is an awful thing, yet I will lie in bed thinking of ways to get rich without doing much. Last week my wife and I dreamed up the idea of opening a bag store, which we would call "It's Your Bag." There is no such store in our area, and isn't it true that people are carrying more on their shoulders? There is the career woman with computer printouts and graphs, the architect with scaled-down blue prints, students with heavier books, bicyclists who need tidy bags to carry tidy lunches. We could do well, we thought. There are more mothers than ever, with diapers popping from purses like stuffing from couches. They will need large shoulder bags. If we were smart, we would jump at this opportunity.

We thought we'd specialize in expensive bags, not straw or plastic ones, unless of course they were stylish. Our bags would be Italian and South American, exotic but practical, clever in a way the can opener was once clever. Men with our fancy travel bags could snicker at those sandwich bags that used to keep their shaver and toothbrush. A woman might shriek with delight, "Where in the world did you get that tote bag?" Her friend, delighted that she had noticed, would shriek back, "I got it at 'It's Your Bag,' and there's a sale going on."

My wife and I dreamed at night when our daughter was asleep. We drew pictures of the 50 x 50 storefront. Shelves would rise along the walls, and the cash register would go near the front, but not too close to the front because shoppers might feel harassed by our greed. We designed our logo: a stork carrying a bag in his bill. There would be classical music, or jazz, and if business was rotten, Little Walter and early Stones. We would open five days a week, would give to charity, and would join the Chamber of Commerce.

That was last week. We dreamed a little in bed, but forgot about our store by lunch time the next day. A bag store would make money, but today I'm thinking that perhaps I could get rich quicker by making beef jerky. Isn't the world in love with salt? I could make the best. Kids would get whiplash pulling on our jerky; truckers would suck on our ant-colored meat and stare at women sitting on bar stools, their beers sending up single-file rows of bubbles. Baseball players would indulge, and men who were really kids at heart would sneak outside after dinner to chew like cows.

Why beef jerky? Because once for Christmas we made a batch in the oven, and a friend, a meat eater who would gladly pull off the flank of a live cow, raved about it.

It's also easy: just buy a thing of meat, go crazy with the salt and pepper, and slide it into the oven.

It's money I want. I rock my wife's hip, say, "Hey, hey, I got an idea." She shows me a red eye and groans. "We can make beef jerky."

I rock her hip again and no life stirs. My mind is alive with schemes. A name for our product slides like mud in my head. I whisper to Carolyn, "We could call it, 'Berjerkly, the meat with a message.' " She groans and shows me her other red eye. "Berkeley is vegetarian," she mumbles, and rolls over. I hadn't thought about it, but it is true.

I persist with my scheme. I tell her we could call it 'smoke dried by the river," even though it would be "oven dried in our kitchen." Who would know and who would care because our jerky would be delicious and a one-of-a-kind treat that would make men cry for their youth. Our jerky would also contain a "little message," a saying from a Chinese philosopher, who would really be me. "Be wise or be foolish, but just be"; "A chair is an upside down forest"; "The river is over there, but who cares?"

I talk to my wife, who feigns sleep and snores fake snores. I pull back her eyelid and her tongue falls out. She knows that I know she's awake. She laughs, and says, rising up on an elbow, that my idea is nonsense, and for me to start the coffee water.

"We can get rich on this one."

"Poor."

"I'm telling you, this is it."

"Poor."

I get out of bed, race on a cold floor to the kitchen to start the coffee, and race back. Carolyn is lying down looking at the ceiling. She pulls crust from the corner of her eye and says, "Maybe I could give cooking lessons."

"Yeah, you could tell people how to make beef jerky."

"No, really."

She is a good cook. Guests have been known to sit down with impeccable table manners, feast on her cooking, rave, and then tip-toe to the kitchen to scrape pots. Yeah, I think, she can give lessons, and I could do my beef jerky, and people would say, "The Sotos really have it together. Look at them make money."

Our daughter would suffer a little. I admit this. Her friends at school would ask, "What does your father do?"

She would try to fall asleep standing up, but her friends would shake her until she *had* to wake up. Dying from embarrassment, she would say, "He owns 'Berjerkly, the meat with a message.' Have you heard of it?" From such experience she would grow up to be a generous person who thinks nothing of money.

The coffee water comes to a boil. My wife, one hand on her bad hip, scoots into her furry slippers that look like dogs with electrified hair, the ones I bought her this past fall when I thought we'd start a shoe store. "Mush," I say to her slippers, "mush, mush." She makes a face at me and ties her robe. Her feet, left over right, start off to the kitchen to grind coffee beans and start breakfast so that I, man of the house, will have the strength to dream of ways to make us rich.

Bag Lunch

We read in the Gospel: "As long as you did it to one of the least of my brothers, you did it to me." A friend of mine believes this. For a year now she's made a bag lunch each day and has taken it out to Grant Street where the Old St. Mary's Church is. A poor person is always there, sitting on the steps, maybe circling like a scrawny pigeon for handouts from the passers-by. She tells me that when she offers her lunch, she almost scares the person, as if it's a fist coming his way, not food. They don't expect such kindness but know what to say: "Thank you," "Bless you, ma'am," "For me? Thank you."

It doesn't take much. Last week I fixed myself a tuna sandwich, with some chips, and a glass of milk. I fixed the same for another, but instead of milk I packed a carton of apple juice, which is more convenient because it's difficult to find those small milks at the store where we shop. I gave my first lunch to a man not far from St. Mary's, but unlike my friend's experience, this man was not surprised when I approached him with lunch. I guess, in a sense, he had been waiting for me.

I've given out about twelve lunches since then, sometimes two a day, and once even three. The hungry are everywhere, within shouting distance—and we live in a good area, a block from Nob Hill and three from the Financial District, where the money easily outnumbers the leaves on a tree. And what have I learned? The poor—the unmistakably homeless in their sad clothes—don't eat their food casually. Often when I offer a lunch, I will walk away to leave them to their meal but have watched (only for a few seconds because I have no right to poke into their personal affairs) them from a distance, and more often than not they will consider each item in the bag: they will bring out the sandwich, the chips, the cookies and juice, savoring the thought of food before they unwrap the sandwich for the first bite. Except that they are outside on a step or a bench, they eat like the rich, who will often glow with pleasure when a waiter serves the entree, comment on its arrangement on the plate, look happy, and then lift a fork to dig in.

I suspect that the poor enjoy sandwiches with meat, not avocado and sprouts, or dates and apple slices, but sandwiches that are fat with wallets of ham and baloney, fried eggs, tuna with onion and chunks of pickles. And if it's apple juice that you give, it should be filtered, not unfiltered like the kind you find at health food stores, mainly because it's clean-looking and more appetizing, not like the dirty water that runs over their feet in the rain.

I have also learned that helping the poor should be a personal matter. I don't think it should be left wholly to the government, nor should it be left to advertisements that read: Sponsor a child for $.50 a day. No doubt if you give in that way a child is helped, maybe even saved from starvation. We should encourage this kind of giving. But we should also encourage individuals to feed the poor hand to hand, not by checks or through institutions, the poor whose faces come up to ours, who are flesh and blood, who talk when we say, "How are you?" As your reward the poor give *you* the occasion to do something for the world. Peter Maurin, one of the founders of *The Catholic Worker* and selfless provider for the poor who, along with Dorothy Day and others, helped found the Houses of Hospitalities, wrote:

18

In the first centuries of Christianity the hungry were fed at a personal sacrifice, the naked were clothed at a personal sacrifice, the homeless were sheltered at a personal sacrifice. And because the poor were fed, clothed, and sheltered at a personal sacrifice, the pagans used to say about the Christians, "See how they love each other." In our own day the poor are no longer fed, clothed and sheltered at a personal sacrifice but at the expense of the taxpayers. And because the poor are no longer fed, clothed and sheltered through personal sacrifice the pagans say about the Christians, "See how they pass the buck."

Peter Maurin—radical Catholic, pacifist, provider for the poor, father to all—also wrote "What we give to the poor is what we carry to the grave." What greater truth are we going to come across today? He himself was a poor man who often slept on benches, in train stations, in borrowed rooms, in friends' houses—all for the sake of the poor so that what he had in the way of money he could give to them. But those were the 30s and 40s. Peter Maurin is dead and buried with no stone to mark his grave. Now it's the 80s with the 90s closing in. How, then, do we find his spirit? We can go outside with a small lunch, pass it on to another, and if someone, baffled by it all, should ask, "Who are you?" you may respond, "I'm that person to whom you give life." Peter Maurin said this, which he learned from Christ. What man or woman would say this is wrong?

Ziggy

He wanted to show me something, this old Confederate son in three sweaters who lived in the same four-cottage complex as my wife and I, a just-married couple settling in with a few sticks of furniture, a kitchen full of wedding gifts, and a new bed that made a *hush* sound when we sat on it. His name was Ziggy, and he was old, a drunk perhaps, and so bored that he even bored me when he passed with a coffee can of water to sprinkle on the drive where no cars parked.

"What is it?" I asked. "Is it about the squash?"

"No."

"Did the melon crack?"

"No, no."

My wife's lucky, I thought. She's at work. She doesn't know the pain of looking at Ziggy's vegetable garden each day; he bends down and shows me the underside of a green-going-to-red tomato. He squashes worms between his fingers, wipes his hands on his can't-bust-'em jeans, and thinks nothing of it.

"Well, what is it?" I asked. "Is it about the mail?"

At least once a week he showed me a piece of misdirected mail for people who had lived in the complex. Some were dead, others moved away, some in the poorhouse like Hank Betzina, who didn't know what to do when his wife died. He shared the stories behind the names, and I, not wanting to be rude, feigned interest and even asked questions. What he did with that mail I never asked.

That morning he had something else for me. He snorted and cleared his throat. He started toward his cottage, an age-peppered hand beckoning me to follow. And I did. I wiped my shoes at his doormat, the letters of welcome nearly rubbed off, and walked in sniffing the air because it smelled of cabbage, or something like cabbage. A quiet fly circled a bare lightbulb in the kitchen.

Ziggy laughed. He asked how old I was. I told him I was twenty-three, and he said he was sixty-eight but felt like a million-year-old wharf rat. He laughed, then wiped his hand across his face and took two steps to the wall, which he slapped with an open palm. The floor began to move—herds of startled cockroaches clicked against each other as they raced from under the couch and armchair.

I stepped back and made an ugly face. Jesus Christ, I thought, and "Jesus Christ," I said as I started toward the door to get the hell out. Ziggy laughed, held my shoulder.

"It's just a joke, boy."

"It's more than a joke," I said, peeling his fingers from my shoulder. "It's sick."

Some of the cockroaches raced into the hallway that led to his bedroom, but most made off to the kitchen, where they hid behind stacks of newspapers and under the water heater and the sink, where the garbage was kept. His apartment once again became very still. The alarm clock buzzed its electronic time and the oscillating fan rattled the newspapers strewn on the coffee table. Ziggy raised a finger before his pursed lips and said, "Shush." He tip-toed in his huge engineer boots to the kitchen and looked over his shoulder at me, his mouth slowly opening to reveal the broken-down fence of gray teeth. He slowly turned his head back around, then jumped as old people jump, stiffly and only a few inches off the floor but high enough to come down and scare the cockroaches back into action. They swarmed from hiding, and Ziggy, quick for an old guy, his eyes shiny with crazed happiness, stepped on as many as he could. He yelled for me to help him, and I just stepped back, horrified. I felt one under my shoe, and still another. I imagined the cockroach thinning to a gray paste under my shoes, and imagined that Ziggy was a year or so away from rooming with Hanka Betzina in the poorhouse.

So that was it, the old growing older. I returned to my cottage and resumed reading Yourcenar's *Hadrian's Memoirs*, and later, when my wife was home, an article on the cockroach in the newspaper. When the bomb falls, the one insect that will remain to multiply and cover the earth with its clicking noise will be the cockroach. There will be no boots, or man laced up in boots, to make them go away.

Starting Young

It was Sue's fault. I was cleaning my bike in the front yard when she came over and said that I could run my hand inside her bra for a quarter plus pull down my pants for her to see. I dropped my rag and asked, "Where do you want to do it?" since I had a quarter, almost a dollar, and I couldn't think of any better way to spend so little money on such a great treat. We thought a minute and then agreed on Mrs. Hancock's shed.

I was scared. I had never touched breasts before and had only dropped my pants for doctors—and they were men, not women, or almost women, like Sue. She was only thirteen but willing to go all the way. When she pulled her panties around her knees, dark hair sprang out like thistles. I looked, bug-eyed, but didn't touch. I thought she might hit me, and I thought it might be dangerous to hit her back because she was a tomboy, tough as three wet cats in a sack, and we'd have to wrestle. I didn't want to tumble around in the shed. There were pitch forks and shovels, a rusty lawn mower sticky with spider webs, and bottles with green liquid. You could get hurt, and maybe even die, in such a shed—and what would Mom think, me dead on the floor with my pants down?

"What do ya wanna do now?" I asked, somewhat bored of looking at her hair.

"I wanna see it, and it won't cost you."

When I showed my penis, which was surrounded by a few renegade hairs, she looked at it for the longest time before she slowly gripped it. It's like a handshake, I thought, like a handshake as she started pulling it up and down. I watched her watch me. The shed creaked; dust motes circled in the shafts of sunlight that slanted in from the broken roof.

Finally when her jerking began to hurt me, I told her to stop. My thing was red, creased where her fingers squeezed. I wiggled up my pants and carefully zipped back up. Now it was my turn. I ran my hand through her bra; her breasts were large and heavy, but I had second thoughts about them being worth a quarter. A look at her slit was worth a quarter, but not the blind push of my hands. Nevertheless I gave her the quarter, and fifteen cents to let me run my hand back and forth across her pantied crotch.

Sue left first, and I followed a few minutes later. I went back to cleaning my bike and that afternoon played baseball in the street, all the time thinking that I had gotten her pregnant. I touched her down there, didn't I, I thought, and maybe I got something inside her. Maybe it was going up there. It doesn't have to go far, does it?

I looked at my hands. There was no stuff on them, but just maybe there was, invisible like germs.

I kept imagining a baby in her arms, baby with my head that was looking right at me. I got scared and played baseball terribly, dropping easy pop-ups and hitting two bouncers to the second baseman, her brother, who kept chattering, "Hey baby, hey baby, hit me one." Surely this was a message.

I felt better, though, when after dinner while we were playing yet another game of baseball, I saw Sue ride by on her bike. She was sucking a popsicle; in her hand she had a bag of sunflower seeds. The money was gone, my quarter and fifteen cents. I felt like I had just gone to confession—great! If she were pregnant and said that I gave her money to let me do it, I would say to her Mom and my Mom, "What money? I got no money!" And she'd have no money to prove anything. She would have already spent it. I was beginning to think like a man.

Shame on us. We start off with quarters and then hide behind dollars when we grow up to cheat when we can.

Taking Inventory of the House

The floor ticks, even when you don't walk on it. The plumbing howls when you place an ear against the wall, and is especially scary when the water heater rumbles into action. During a heavy storm the windowpanes drip black tears that puddle near the stereo, which, if it's on, is turned low so as not to disturb those in the house, namely wife and daughter and cat Pip, who, at this moment, is sleeping with her legs shot straight up in the air, lips curled into that perpetual feline smile.

The oak dining table stands on three legs and is surrounded by four chairs. Two framed pictures, one of Roman ruins and the other a Georgia O'Keeffe print, hang on the wall. Both are dusty; both are faded from the sun which, during summer, angles in at about eight-thirty and stays until ten. Chinese paper devil masks, also faded, ring the space between the windows and ceiling. They are ferocious-looking and ominous and lordly, but under them our family, not in the least disturbed, eats its meals in great oily slurps and thinks nothing of death.

The living room contains a couch, a rug with meaningless designs like the shapes of germs under a microscope, two lamps, a basket for old newspapers, a basket for receipts from restaurants, car repairs, and the like, and shelves of unevenly shaped books. One of the books, *Asian Figures*, has the aphorism: "Spit straight up and learn something," which is responsible for the stains along the wall. When the father read it to the daughter at dessert time, she laughed so hard that the juice she had in her mouth spurted from her nostrils. This made her cry; this made her drop her cookie, which the cat carried away in the corner of its mouth. But the daughter is not here just now. If she were, she might be seated on the couch taking a spelling test for which she will receive a pinto bean from her father. This is no game but life itself. She needs five hundred to get a horse; she's earned over two hundred and her father, now a little uncertain about what he's started, has slowed spelling tests to one a week.

The bedrooms are small, seemingly tidy, but dusty in all corners, with sickle-shaped toenails, dead moths, hair let loose from all places, and wadded kleenex and scribbled telephone messages that linger for weeks, scattered here and there.

The parents' bedroom: swivel lamps on the wall, drawers, a queen-size bed that's really more like a king size, for the parents are small as piss ants. There is a glass of stale water on a small blue night stand which, if opened, would reveal cosmetics, a hand mirror with a kiss of volcano-red lipstick on it, mismatched earrings, and classy perfumes, none of which were presents from the husband. There is also a pipe-cleaner sculpture titled "Troubled Kite," which is a tangled mess that represents a kite that has had the misfortune of falling on a power line; the daughter made it in kindergarten and earned not one, but three beans. There are also framed portraits of the parents that the daughter did in the first grade. One reads "I am Mom" and is a crayoned picture of the mother seen from the kid's view: her nostrils are large and black and her arms are like clubs. The other reads "Me and Dad Practicing Tae Kwon Do" and is a picture of the daughter and father, glasses bent on his grinning face of yellow teeth and stand-up hair, in fighting position.

The daughter's room has just been cleaned. On any other day her toys, mostly stuffed animals, would lie scattered on the floor. Her one plant that was given to her to encourage responsibility is dead, crisp as a bowl of corn flakes, and her cat, just a while ago asleep in the living room, is now sitting wide awake on top of the piano, among karate trophies, books, and hair ribbons and Hello Kitty make-up kits and combs. And there is a desk along the wall that looks out onto the side of the house, where the family grows Early Girl tomatoes and unruly berries. The desk is a student desk, and the books on top of it have nothing to do with school: they're library books about girls from the country who ride horses and hate boys.

The kitchen is painted pumpkin-color, is warm, and is clean though cluttered with pots and a rack of washed cups and dishes. The one plant, given to the wife from the husband, is doing well on the windowsill. There is a dead fly, with its legs in the air, right next to the plant. No one is permitted to wipe it away because the father has an experiment going: he wants to discover what happens to a dead fly. Over the years he has whacked many with rolled newspapers and let them quiver and die on the floor, and has always wanted to keep track of their progress but for one reason or other never has. Now it is time. It's been there three weeks and the only visible change is that it has grown paler and has moved clockwise, just slightly, which the father has attributed to wind that leaks in from the window.

The father is just now in the kitchen, along with the wife who is on her knees, basting a turkey that's the color of a baseball mitt, short legs pointing upward. He asks, very seriously, "You mean you don't believe in sock cannibalism?" He has been reading an article in the Sunday paper about a researcher who over a thirteen-month period has studied "missing sock syndrome"—or, in the other words, the socks we lost between the time they are washed and dried to the time the folding begins. They disappear, inexplicably, and are no doubt a cause of some family feuds across America. "What the hell did you do with your socks? I swear," a mother yells, and the kid, maybe crying, maybe wishing his mother dead, says, "I don't know. Don't blame me." No, we shouldn't blame the kid but the dryer, which has eaten the lost sock, the researcher (on a government grant) argues, and the father, one of the few who still believes in the spirit of the Guardian Angels, sides with the researcher since a number of his socks have disappeared without a clue, and he certainly was not to blame.

The wife shoves the turkey back in, refills her wine glass, and asks, "Where do you get this stuff?"

"Honey," he coos, "honey, honey, it's all true." He takes her by the waist, presses his nose, which is the color of a turkey before it goes into the oven, into her neck. They kiss and then part to drink wine. Their daughter, who is at the kitchen table coloring a fresco (for which she will earn a bean) from the Sistine Chapel in a coloring book from the Museum of Modern Art, says, "Dad, let's get back to reality."

He downs his wine, licks the rim of the glass, and says, "Ok, I will"—and begins talking about the fifth dimension which, he believes, is that howling noise we hear when we place an ear against wood—tables and walls—and sometimes our very own mattress, if we lie very still and think powerful thoughts.

Evening Walk

Whenever I announce after dinner that we're going for a walk my daughter runs to the back yard to busy herself with a handful of sand and leaves and things of that sort. I get up slowly from the couch, tired but knowing very well that a walk is what I need. I run a hand across my wife's rump as I pass her at the kitchen sink, dear wife elbow deep in soap suds. She offers a quick cynical smile, as if to say, "You lazy bum, where are you going?"

The problem with an evening walk is that I talk a lot. I don't know when to be quiet. My daughter will start off at my side as together we admire gardens for what they are, alive or nearly alive with flowers, but half-way around the block and up Francis Street, she'll skip a few steps ahead because I will say things like, "That tree is older than your grandma, but not by much. Did you know they put her in the concentration camp during the war, and Mommie would have had to go there too except Grandpa was fighting in Europe. I bet you didn't know that?"

In the back yard I find Mariko trying to piece together an apple that had fallen from the tree. She shows me the two halves. Strange, I think, I've never seen this happen—an apple split nearly perfectly in half. She tries to involve me in solving this phenomenon, and in fact I start talking about a baseball bat that once split right in two on a sissy hit to second base. Then I catch on; she's avoiding the walk.

"Let's go, kid," I tell her, and place the apple on a lawn chair, and together we start up the block around the corner and before you know I'm saying things like, "When I was a kid I picked grapes. Do you like grapes? Well it's a hard life cutting grapes. Hours and hours of work and the people who pick them don't get paid very much. My grandma used to do that kind of work, and my mom, and your uncles and aunt."

Mariko skips ahead with a branch she's picked up from the gutter. She doesn't want to hear it. I don't want to hear it either, but I think she has to know about difficult lives. She's a little girl with a piano and stuffed animals and three meals a day and snacks in fancy wrappers. Perhaps I'm an ogre about what I think is my duty, to explain the unjust world, just as when I tried to get her a head start on others by demanding that she know her colors just about the time she began to talk in sentences. I would pull up a handful of grass and ask, "What color?" *Green*. "And this?" pointing to the rose. *Pink*. "My face?" *Brown*. "And my teeth?" tapping the front ones with a finger. *Orange*.

Darn kid, I remember laughing to myself. She's going to be a wise-guy.

I also thought it was my duty to tell her about Christ by saying a bed-time prayer. I didn't know that in the dark when I kissed her and she would say, "Kiss Dolphy too," her stuffed animal that she loves dearly, that she would turn him over and let me kiss his butt—or whatever it is that a dolphin has. She would laugh, and I thought it was out of happiness that she was discovering Christ.

Actually she's very sweet, shy to the point of rudeness, and doesn't need to be lectured to. She eats everything off her plate, prays, offers toys to friends because she loves them. She cries at movies and feels sorrow for characters in her books, and is eager to be held in our arms and would hold us—mommie and daddy—if she had the strength to pick us up.

31

Nevertheless, there's still that chance she'll grow up unappreciative. It's a father's duty to scare children out of their wits. "When I was a kid I fought Okies with my bare hands." I laugh at this one, and she wrinkles her face, obviously disturbed that she should have to hear such trivia. "I sold pop bottles to buy my candy, and your uncle once broke his arm but didn't get to the doctor until we sold our furniture." I laugh at this, partly because it's true (my dumb brother dared Eddie King, a mean kid in a striped T-shirt, to run over his arm by lying on the sidewalk with an outstretched arm) and partly because I catch myself embroidering the past. Actually, we didn't have to sell our furniture, but we did wait a few days. Poor brother. That first night our Mom tied two ice cubes in a wash cloth for his "hurt," closed the bedroom door on Rick to let him moan and cry, and let me taunt him for being a big baby.

"Some kids had to walk through snow," I tell her, hearing in the back of my head our step-father, drunk at the kitchen table and repeating his stories. "Knew a kid who was picked up by a tornado, and a girl who was carried away by a pit bull. In my time, you had to be tough just to get to school."

When my story telling gets louder, Mariko begins to skip fast, not looking back, and I start walking faster, telling her about pickle barrels we stood in when we were kids. She's now running, the leafy stick in her hand fluttering like greenfire, because the corner is up ahead and an evening without me—and my stories—can't be far beyond.

Scary

It's no use. The world is a dark place. I drink thick coffee, read books, and poke the fire that smolders with a wet log, the embers blinking like a dark closet of cats. I'm reading theology, Lady Julian of Norwich and hell-flaming warnings from the New Testament. I'm reading the prophesies about the coming world that will drown the sinner and throw life boats to the good. In short, I'm trying to scare myself, which is something I seldom get to do now that I'm an adult.

And now it's time. My family is gone, it's raining, and our cat Pip is sniffing a raw wound on her neck. I go to my drawer. The gun, a .38, is there, heavy as a stone, cold as a stone, oily in an oily flannel cloth. I take the bullets out, stand them up, and am amazed how each reminds me of a chapel. They don't really look like chapels, but I think to myself, "Chapels, they look like little chapels." I leave the bullets on the nightstand, but take the gun to the living room where I stand at the front window and look out. Although it is dusk and raining, a man is raking leaves. His face is the color of mud, his coat like leaves at his feet. He stops and looks up. A car passes with only its parking lights on, yellow slants that strike me as sinister. I watch the car disappear and catch myself breathing hard. I go back to the bedroom for the bullets and return to the living room to read C. S. Lewis and his view on miracles. It's very dense, like the rain itself, which is coming down harder and rushing in stick-choked gutters. I put the book down. I turn off the lamp; the room darkens, though I can still see puffs of black uncurling from the smoldering fire. I can see my cat asleep near the furnace, a rattling noise issuing from her throat when she exhales.

I get up and start the coffee water. I wash my hands at the sink. A branch waves in front of the kitchen window. Except for the hiss of gas from the stove's burners, it's absolutely quiet. I think of the gun on the coffee table. It could make things unquiet. I could fire it into the couch, which may or may not bring the police. But my story is ready: "Officer, I was cleaning the gun when it misfired. I'm sorry to have caused so much trouble." I could poke a finger in the hole in the couch where the bullet entered, and poke a finger in the hole where the bullet exited and entered the wall. "See, no one is dead." I would laugh, poke the fire, and listen to my cat hiss behind the curtain.

But I don't fire the gun. I brew coffee instead, lace it with half and half, and return to the living room where I watch the fire blink its smoldering embers. I get up when the phone rings. There's no one on the other end, just a distant sea-howl. I slowly place the receiver down. I go to the window and watch the man who was raking leaves lift a plastic bag awkwardly into his arms. He boosts it into his pick-up. He tosses his rake back there too, stomps his boots, blows into his cupped hands, and goes inside.

A car passes, then another. The paperboy is stopped by a man in a baseball cap. They talk, point to the end of the street, and leave together. I turn away, put on a Jessie Norman record of German lieders, and open the phone bill: there's a call to Paris? I'm thinking of my friend Wolfgang in Austria when the phone rings again. I pick up the receiver with one hand, and hold the gun with the other. It's a friend asking about a book, and I tell him that I don't have the book. He asks if I want to see a movie, and I tell him I don't have time

34

to see a movie, hang up, and return to the living room to drink my coffee, which is now cold but not so cold as to ruin everything. I ball up a newspaper and toss it into the fire; the newspaper bursts into flames, and I think of the great war ahead, friends who will go insane and bite their arms like dogs and look right into the flash.

I like it when I'm alone. It gives me time to think. My life is half over, my wife's life is half over. The world is going to roll over and sink like a freighter. There's nothing like scaring yourself to round out the day.

Spring Break

We woke up in a parked car that we borrowed to sleep in because we had no place to stay, little money, and reasoned that anyone who owned a Volkswagon bug with a space sign on the back window would understand our plight. It was 1969, and hippies—or people who looked like hippies—with their beads, long hair, patchouli oil-stench, were everywhere—and Richard and I were on spring break from high school.

We had hitchhiked from Fresno (with our own beads around our necks), and it had taken two days to get to San Francisco. We had slept in vineyards, cowered from eggs hurled at us from passing cars, winced at dust, stood in boredom reading the same message on the back of a stop sign: Billy Loves His Baby.

I had never slept sitting up before and mumbled "How do you feel, man?" when I woke feeling like a couple thousand dollars worth of shit. I poked a red eye at Richard, who was in the front seat, and he showed me his jelly-red eyes and a yellow tongue as he began to laugh from feeling bad.

We got out of the car. It was not yet morning; the street lights, blue against the bruise-blue sky, were still on. In the distance, a garbage truck whined its elephant noise. We rolled our sleeping bags and started walking with no idea where we were going. Within five blocks we were dead tired. We sat down, looked around stupidly with our mouths open, and walked some more. Is this what it's like to be a hippie? neither one of us said but thought. The beads around our necks clinked softly with each step.

It was just getting light when we found a small park where we unraveled our sleeping bags in a row of bushes and tried to sleep. But pesky flies, loosened from God knows what dog turds, began to pester us with their noise and pinching bites. When we couldn't stand it any more, we sat up, cussed, and dragged our sleeping bags onto the lawn where we watched the day come to life: the cars, hurrying people, children on the way to school, hippies (like us) coming out of the bushes with their dogs who wore hippie bandanas themselves.

We had $.65 pancakes for breakfast, and glasses of water, before we walked down to Fisherman's Wharf to ride a ferry around the Bay. It was $3.50 for an hour tour, and $5.00 for two hours. We chose the two-hour tour because anyone could see that it was the better deal, money-wise. At first we got a kick out of the rocking motion, and the wind, and the salt spray, and a gull with one hypnotic eye soaring alongside the boat, and islands, hazy in the distance but coming into view. In half an hour we were thoroughly bored by the bay cruise: the monotonous rolling motion and the wind and sea and the same stupid sea gull trying to shit on us. Richard, yellow tongue jumping up and down in his mouth, laughed, "I'm so bored I think I'm dead."

I was bored, then mad when I saw the hour-long ferry we could have taken if we hadn't been so greedy begin its slow turn and start back to the wharf. I yelled at Richard, and he punched me in the arm, "You're the one who said 'Let's go for two hours.' " To top it off, there was a group of junior high kids up the railing space up front. They let loose crazed laughter each time a wave blasted them. I wanted to stand up there and be splashed with a vigorous wave, but they wouldn't make room for us.

Luckily Richard dropped a quarter between the slats on the deck, which gave us something to do. With dirty fingers and two toothpicks salvaged from an ashtray, we managed to retrieve the quarter and felt good about erasing thirty minutes from the cruise.

After the ferry ride we returned to the park to lean (hippie style) against our sleeping bags and eat the oranges we had taken from our backyard at home for the trip. They were good, and a lead-in to an afternoon of open conversation. What's your favorite fruit? Pomegranates and pineapple. What's your favorite book? *To Sir with Love* and *The Prophet*. The worst thing you've ever done? Put a cat in a dryer and punch a brother's stomach where he had stitches from an appendectomy. He also told me that his older brother Marty used to hang his wife upside down from a window. I nibbled on a peel and said that was pretty bad. Years later when I met his brother and his wife, I could only picture her hanging upside down, her dress like a limp parachute worked up around on her face as she mumbled "Please, Marty, let me go."

We walked around, feeling better after the oranges and the sunflowers seeds we had bought, thinking all the while that we looked pretty cool with our sleeping bags and the filthy hippie-look that began to shine in our shoulder-length hair. We stayed another day, mostly watching people give us peace signs which we returned, along with smiles. Then we hitchhiked back home in a record speed of six hours, repeatedly giving peace signs. Peace to the Dodge Dart. Peace to the Cadillac and the Ford Falcon. Peace to our brothers stranded on the side of the road, thumbs out, and peace to our senior citizens in the large boat-like Imperial living it up with thermo-cups of coffee.

Let out at the Olive Street exit, we walked six miles home feeling pretty good, then great when we reached Richard's house and his parents were not home to make noises about how dirty we looked. We fixed sandwiches, which we ate in his room, and silently played with our beads, the ones we had taken with us on the trip and the ones we had bought, while we listened to Eric Burdon say over and over "Monterrey, Monterrey. Yeh. Yeh, down in Monterrey."

After an hour of this the magic was gone; we were in Fresno, not San Francisco. I had to get home. When Richard gave me a peace sign, I said "fuck you" and punched him in the stomach where his stitches would be if he had been his brother. He laughed and let his yellow tongue jump around in his mouth. We were the best of friends.

Pip

What does our cat do behind our backs? We wake up very slowly, neither of us willing to brave the cold floor, and walk over and turn on the furnace. I have one, possibly two cups of coffee, help our daughter search for matching socks, and watch my wife slip into three different dresses, unhappy with them all. I also let in our cat, who meows "Ma Ma." My wife, with a new scarf the color of a parrot, falls into the morning game, asks, "Yes, daughter?" Pip, her other daughter, saunters to her bowl in the laundry room. It's empty, or nearly empty. She looks up at me and cries, "Ma Ma." I pour her crunchies, pluck a leaf from her back, and return to the bedroom to get dressed.

The coffee is drunk, the sock found, the dress that was ugly on Tuesday is suddenly gorgeous on Thursday—and we're off for the day, leaving behind our cat who, once fed, is thrown out again. She watches us drive away, mouth shut, her whiskers already beaded with rain that's coming down harder.

What do they do while we are gone? I know that dogs bark a lot behind fences, sleep, dig up the yard with their snouts and paws, and sometimes run away to sniff new-mowed lawns. And running away, they often get lost, so that later a parent, with a child tagging along with tacks or a stapler, will post flyers and distribute them to neighbors. Only last week I saw such a flyer on a telephone pole. The family was seeking a Labrador who responds to the name "Jimmy" or "Jim." He was described as "yellow, forty pounds, with collar." There was a photograph of him holding a frisbee, or was it his dish? I couldn't tell because the flyer was fuzzy, rain-streaked, and torn.

As a kid I often let my dog do as he pleased, and once this was a mistake because he found me on the Fresno Mall while I was trying to romance my first girl with a coke and a box of popcorn. My date and I had run out of things to say and were just sitting, she looking at the fountain, which was polluted with popcorn boxes, and me gazing at the clothes at Walter Smith, when I felt a moist touch, which I thought was my girl's hand. Had she become romantic? I turned around. No, it was my dog's snout, and his tongue was licking my salty knuckles. The girl turned and sort of screamed, "Oh, a dog!" I shoved Brownie away, yelled "Get, get outta here, dog. Who do you think you are?" Well, for one, he was my dog, and two he was in big trouble with me because I had warned him time and time again not to wander.

Brownie only looked up at me with watery eyes, paws pressed sweetly together, and whined for food. I didn't know what to do. He was ruining everything. I poured the popcorn kernels onto the ground for Brownie to gobble while we got away. But he caught up with us and for the rest of the afternoon tagged along, giving a new meaning to the phrase *ménage a trois*.

But what does our cat do while we are gone? The days I stay home, I notice that she mostly sleeps and eats, plays with balls of lint, and walks from room to room in search of a warm lap. I've also noted that cats blink a lot, squint their eyes dreamily, and smile their cat smiles for no reason at all. This is scary; it's an inner light that comes on, along with— who knows—maybe sitar music inside their heads.

I know what we *do* to cats. For her science project, our daughter kept a graph to see what Pip "purrferred" in terms

41

of drink. Mariko set bowls of white wine, water, milk, and chocolate milk on the kitchen floor, and had me read the newspaper, like it was a typical night, so that Pip would not get suspicious that something was up. When Pip was let in, she ran to the kitchen, looked around, said, "Ma Ma," and began to lick and bite under her leg. When Mariko, scientist with her own conclusions, opened the refrigerator, Pip jumped up and poked her head inside. In the end, we concluded that she has a poor sense of smell, eats by habit, and is not too bright.

This morning we drove off and left Pip in the rain to let her swim and creep for life, as Smart of his Jeffery. I went to campus to baffle my students about an obscure poem; Mariko went to school to master cursive writing; Carolyn went off to edit an art book. I like to think that Pip went off to bring down a bird, thump it out with another cat in the bushes, lurk in trees, chase leaves, run between cars, sleep like a stone, and hang on wires for precious life—which for her comes in a set of nine—with a tail that stands up to greet us when we come home with warm hands and a bag of rattling food.

How We Stand

"I'm the best of the worst," our daughter says of her P.E. class. I toss the tennis ball and it passes through her hands. She races for it, bends, and throws like a girl; the ball kicks off my hand and races away like a mouse. Our daughter, as it happens, is not very athletic, with little muscle, no aggression, and no sense of winning. She enjoys play, not games, and I'm happy about this.

"I was the worst of the best in my days," I tell her, which may or may not be true. Perhaps I was among the best of the worst, those weak but game kids who were chosen to be on teams, just before the sissies and the fat kids who always stood in right field, away from the action, with their pudgy hands at their sides. I was small for my age, not quick, not threatening, not strong enough to put fear in an outfielder's life, but happy to play, and only slightly insulted not being the first chosen.

Kickball in elementary years, baseball in junior high, wrestling in high school and now karate in my middle-years. On occasion, at our studio, we choose sides to spar. Nothing has changed. I'm chosen somewhere near the end, just before the out-of shape green belt with poor kicks and the lowly yellow belt with no defense except his rank (we're told not to hurt beginners). And my trophies bear out the truth: second place for kata, third place for 30 & Over, fourth place for

43

fighting, first place for kata in which there were only five participants, two of them senior citizens, and so on. The trophies sit in the attic, waist deep in pink insulation.

My racquetball trophies mean very little to my heart. They're stored in a workbench out in the yard, in fact they mean less to me than my 100% score on my driver's license, and my 120/60 blood pressure, and the fortune cookie that insisted *You are a man of courage*. Yes and no. I once crossed a busy New York street, at 5 o'clock, and lived. But a busy street hardly counts. It's my athletic prowess, my desire just to be somewhere in the middle, that counts.

Now our daughter. She's the best of the worst, among the last chosen for kickball, right before the fat girl in a plaid dress that's like a barrel pulled up high around her waist. What's mildly troubling to me is that she takes it in stride, pleased just to be on a team and relieved to play a position where the ball never rolls. She's not in the least hurt that she's no good at sports, that she's eight years old and can't ride a bike or catch a ball without opening her mouth in fear, or roller skate without falling every third stride.

But this is only mildly troubling, and only when I think that she'll have to contend with the physical world. In fact, I'm pleased that she's not competitive because the last thing we need is another kid who wants to be first, a winner, a hot shot trying to catch her breath at the finish line, under a hoop, or home plate; someone with first place trophies sitting on a mantle, gleaming like stolen goods for attention. I like her how she is, shy and wimpy, with her real life taking place inside her head.

I'm pleased that she never thinks of me, her father and provider for the family, as athletic, though we do watch our share of sports on television, mainly boxing and football. She has never said, "Dad, are you any good at karate? If you were really, really mad at Jessica's father, do you think you could beat him up?" which at a different time, in the 50s and 60s, might have been a relevant question for a kid to ask. I don't know what I would say; perhaps I would offer a wimpy answer about peace in the world, love, kindness toward all others, even your enemy. Maybe I would make a fist and predict, "Lights out for that sucker."

But she won't ask that question. She'll play with me for a while with an orange tennis ball, and talk about her friends, all of them gone for the weekend; talk about her teacher, a book she's reading, her favorite dessert. When I toss the ball, her mouth drops open, and her eyes grow large with disbelief that the ball is actually arching toward her and maybe, maybe not, fall into her hands.

Moses

    I'm thinking of my friend's collie, Moses, and the evenings when a group of us guys sat in back yards to talk big talk—women who refused us by leaving curt messages on answering machines, and magazine editors, blind to our talent, who returned our poems, unread. Moses would join us by sitting some distance away under the dead apricot tree, his paws pressed sweetly together, his head poised and utterly dignified. Of course, he didn't join our conversation; he was too smart for that. We were full of nonsense about the opposite sex, and full of beer, which made us stupid by the time the night was over.

    Chris, Jon, Omar, me. At dusk we barbecued chicken on a hibachi. This was what we could afford, and tomatos from the garden, squash, brown rice left over from the time a girlfriend moved out. It was a poor man's club, four guys and a dog who snapped buttered bread when we flung it into the air; a dog who nibbled at rinds of fat with better manners than any of us; a dog who licked his lips, delicately, before he barked his approval to Jon the cook. He barked, wagged his tail, and sat watching us drink ourselves into a confessional mood that let our deepest fears spill out, like mine, which is that we will not be able to walk around when we die, and Jon's, which is that we will walk around when we die.

    But before we arrived at that drunken state, we talked,

ate, maybe played bocce ball under the grape arbor, maybe even argued until we wanted to thump it out on the lawn. And just what did we say about women? Well, for one, "What can we do? You can't live with them and you can't live without them." "Oops," one would say when a lover's period was two weeks late. Being sensitive guys, we took sips of beer, reflected on the stars and the blinking lights of passing jets in the night sky, and peed horse splashes along the fence, being too tired or drunk or despicable to use the bathroom.

Moses was a civil being. If he could have talked, he would have told us about the female, told us, for instance, how to race for her without breathing hard, how to walk side by side without stepping on her toes, how to live with her without farting too crudely. When a female dog passed the house, Moses would get up, ears of corn, and trot over to sniff her nose to nose, nose to rump, and nibble and playfully growl under her collar.

He was a dog for us all. What child would not run a hand through his dusty fur and feel a warmth? What grandpa would not go to a knee and remember his youth? Even a mother, coming home with bags of groceries, would stop and go through her bags until she found the cookies. What man or woman, child or adult, could claim such love?

Moses was also better looking than any of us. Orange fur, sad eyes of a French actor, snout like a party hat, nimble paws, nimble gait, up and down teeth that were white and seemingly unused. The four of us? Bald, or nearly bald, heavy and skinny legged, saggy in the face and ugly in the mouth, even when it was closed. He was perfect in his fur, in his role as a dog, and we were imperfect in our flesh, in our role as humans, for we had only a splatter of gray intelligence inside the head. His role was to knock over garbage cans, look out the window, race to the kitchen when the refrigerator was opened, be petted by children, nose the skirts of our women friends, who would shriek and yell, "You nasty dog!"

Somehow we could never understand our roles as men. Should we marry, stay married; kill or be killed; find jobs, or wait for the phone to ring and a voice to say on the other end, "Mr. Veinberg, we have lots of money for you." We were unsure what to do with our lives. We thought we should write for a living, but could never find that person who would give money for poems.

A few days after one of these back yard barbecues, Moses was hit by a car, returned home limping on three legs, and died breathing shallow sighs, his soft eyes blinking less and less until they stopped altogether. He went like my childhood dog, Blackie, with little fuss, with little noise about how he did no wrong in his years. His fur wavered in the breeze. He became heavy when we held him in our arms, this old dog with nothing in his bones.

The earth is richer because of Moses, buried not "gallantly with his feet straight up in the air," as a poet friend remarked, but buried lying on his side. It's a long blackness in the earth; we must find a comfortable position to wait it out.

Feeling Normal

I'm unrepentant on a park bench. For every attractive woman who passes, two bad thoughts knock on my forehead and enter, lie down and frolic with a bold nakedness that scares me. It's lunch time, the sun half-hidden behind clouds but bright enough to do tricks to my senses, and the women, some alone, some in pairs, some in packs, are so beautiful that tears, like a leaky faucet, drip inward. They're unobtainable and, because of that, more desirable, mysterious, dangerous—all the qualities a man builds into what he can't have.

I only have to glance at the woman across from me, glance and look away, and the knocking begins. Her knees are pink, her cheeks pink, her nails a shade of pink, and so it must be that behind her career woman's clothes—the little gray pin-stripe suit—she must be pink. Gray and pink. I like those colors, and black too, the color of her briefcase, which winks a yellow light on the brass latches each time she opens it to ruffle through papers. I have to wonder to myself, is that the signal? Would she like me to get up and move closer to her, sit, right next to her? The latches wink, go dead, wink again.

On lunch break she's taking in the sun, no doubt tired of closed-in office smells of xerox machines and typewriters and greasy phones. Maybe she's a lawyer, an accountant perhaps, someone in merchandising. Whatever she does she seems

49

happy to be outside eating her lunch. She has already finished her sandwich and is now enjoying her peach. She takes a small bite, chews, and runs a slow tongue across her teeth, which seem also to wink with the noontime light. What would Freud say about that? What would my mother say, a young woman like that chewing so lasciviously?

But how should I approach her? What would I say? Hello, this is Mr. Irresistible. Yes, I am an Aries. Pink and gray are my favorite colors. My BMW is in the shop. I could tell her, "I'm from Fresno!" which would lead smoothly right into my saying that they grow peaches there and that the one she is eating is probably from my hometown, was in fact picked by someone I know. Who would ever guess that we had something in common?

Love can start harmlessly, over lunch for instance, and grow into hand-holding walks and dinner. Maybe we can go out tomorrow night, try the Emerald Garden, yet another new Vietnamese restaurant on California. And the Lumiere is just down the street from there. We can see a movie, see ourselves in the movie: I'm the lead actor in a wheelchair, some unfortunate fellow who was pushed under a train by a psychotic; she's the nurse on the nightshift whose real interest is not the sick but literature, and she is, in fact, 13 units away from a second degree, this time in English. Together we fall for one another, but not after some jealous rage at a restaurant. I stir my bread pudding into mush when she hints that she has been married before, two times in fact, OK, if you really want to know the truth, three times; she smacks my face when I mention an old love has better teeth.

But I'm going to meet this woman. I've been working out at the Y, and I'm sweaty, sour as a dirty sock, and generally bad to look at. I'm also hungry for lunch, and married, and a father to a great child who's learning about Europe this week. Why should I ruin myself, and others? And what right does this other woman have to enter my life and cause havoc?

Shouldn't a single woman know better? And the truth of the matter is that I have to hurry home: jog a little, walk; jog a little, walk. I have to answer a letter and start the stew my wife expects when she comes home, tired of the office smells she endures daily. If it weren't for the sun, none of this enticement would happen. It would be too dreary for these women to leave their work place ten minutes early and return ten minutes late. They would not swagger by in tight skirts, each new skirt more beautiful. Neither would bad thoughts knock on my forehead, enter and frolic on all fours. No brass latches would wink and tell me "Go ahead, make a fool of yourself, and tell me you're an unmarried Aries with money and kindness and humor and health." And that would be too bad.

The Occasional Movie Reviewer

After doing the laundry, some letter writing, I answered the phone, my wife calling to ask if I wanted long envelopes or short ones. I changed into a heavy sweater, which is what you need in summer in San Francisco, and took the cable car that runs outside our apartment to the Lumiere to take in a matinee, which is something I never do because it cuts into the day.

The movie was *Sincerely Charlotte*, a French film, and unlike the French movies that I've seen in the past, this one made sense. Its theme was well known: an old girlfriend (Charlotte) comes back to haunt her former lover (Mathieu). Mathieu is a musician with long scraggly hair, a day-old beard, and bags under his eyes which are quiet and reflective. He looks at a wine glass, and he grows *quiet*, scratches his whiskers, and runs his hand through his hair. He picks up his violin, sighs, and becomes *reflective* as he looks at a sinkful of dirty dishes. He scratches his beard, turns to his wife, who suspects something is up, to say "No" when she asks if anything is wrong. He again runs his hands through his hair, which I notice for the first time is greasy.

His old love takes refuge in the study behind his house, where she cries a lot, smokes cigarettes, looks at old photographs of them—Charlotte and Mathieu—in their bloom of first love, and then throws them aside to give a moment or two to Bernard, her deceitful lover and not very talented writer, whom she has killed. She has more cigarettes and eats a whole chunk of bread that is offered to her when Mathieu visits her in the middle of the night. Do they make love? No. Do they want to make love? Yes and no. There's one dead body in the way, and two live ones sleeping only a hundred feet away—his wife, whom he loves dearly, and a child from her first marriage. It's morally wrong to make love, their eyes, now more quiet and reflective than ever, tell each other, and they decide instead just to make out for a while. Finally Mathieu returns to his bedroom and his wife, whose hip he rocks tenderly with the hand that has momentarily let go of his hair, before he rolls over to sleep.

The next morning his wife and her child, whom he loves dearly, go off to play tennis, which allows Charlotte the chance to leave the study to take a long, hot bath, while Mathieu paces the floor downstairs, wondering to himself what this all means. For the first time (illumination) I discover that Charlotte is pretty: light freckles on her face and shoulders, small, manageable breasts, short hair like a boy's, and a slight overbite that makes my throat itch. She steps out of the bath, islands of soapsuds sliding down her body, and pats herself dry. I like that. And I like it that she's perky, playful, and apparently not bad with a gun. Perhaps it's also a good time to explain that Mathieu doesn't know that Charlotte has killed her lover. He knows that something is wrong, but not horribly wrong. When he finds out (a newspaper falls from a fellow musician's lap and a picture of Charlotte stares right at him), he runs out of a recording session, no doubt jeopardizing his career, which has brought him a large house in Paris and a new wife and a child.

They are in the study. Darkness plays in the corners. Charlotte explains in a flashback that she had gone to snoop on her lover, who had failed to show up at one of her night club acts (did I mention she was a singer?), and discovers a bitchy American in her lover's living room. She throws her out, then turns to Bernard to exchange nasty words, leaves, and later returns to argue some more, only to discover that there is no one to argue with: Bernard is dead, apparently a suicide.

Mathieu asks, "Is it true?" Charlotte inhales her cigarette and says, "No. But does it sound good?" At about this point in the movie Mathieu's wife, whose name I've already forgotten, begins to get suspicious. It seems that some of her panties have disappeared, and a bra, and yes, one of her coats. She pushes a finger into her chin, which is pretty tight for an old girl, and wonders. She decides to see if by chance they're in Mathieu's study—and sure enough they are, along with a note to Mathieu from Charlotte. What's going on, she wonders and, later, when her husband returns home, says quietly, with the greatest tact and reason, "My flower panties disappeared last night. Do you know about this?" Mathieu pours himself a drink and says, "What are you saying?"

It's then that I begin to think that Paris is in many ways like my hometown, Fresno, where there's often a weekend shooting brought about by jealousy and too much drinking. But unlike Paris, Fresno is mean. A wife will lack understanding. She'll shout a little bit, maybe cry and peek between her fingers at her husband, and then in the middle of the night, beat him (he'll be drunk from too many suds) with a heavy glass ashtray. This happened to my uncle; it took him two days to remember his name, and a week to get back onto his feet.

But back to the movie. In spite of her tears the wife is full of understanding when Mathieu tells her that he's going to take a few days off from violin playing to drive Charlotte to the Spanish border because she's broke and needs help. They drive slowly, and make love slowly, which is lucky for me because once again I get to see the freckles on her shoulders, which are round as stones but soft.

The movie races along at full speed: on their way to Spain they steal a car, they get in an accident that showers glass all over them, she seduces a truck driver for a wad of money (I never knew that French currency was so large), and they escape from two motorcycle cops. And resting at a woodsy cottage only two miles from the Spanish border, Mathieu's wife, whom he loves dearly, shows up with her child. The movie slows: some violins start in and the light gets soft. The lake laps at the shore, and birds, Spanish sparrows I guess, bicker over some twigs. The wife is again understanding, and so is Charlotte, who finally sees that she's in the way. While Mathieu and his wife talk under a tree, their eyes quiet and reflective, Charlotte hops onto a bike and makes her way to a highway. Mathieu discovers her absence, asks the child, who is playing with a tub of water and a bracelet that sparkles CHARLOTTE, where she has gone, and then runs up the path calling her name. At the highway he spots the bike, one tire spinning lazily, searches the road, and chases the truck that he sees Charlotte get in, but to no avail.

Two years later: We see Mathieu and his wife, whom he loves dearly, carrying a baby swaddled up to its throat in blankets and her child from her first marriage, boarding a train for a week on the beach somewhere. As the train pulls out, we see another train and, who would believe it, it's Charlotte behind one of the windows. She waves, rolls down her window, waves some more, and calls "Cousin, cousin dear!" as she doesn't want to let on to her husband, who is older and richer, that they were once lovers. Mathieu's eyes grow quiet and no doubt his heart slows down like an old alarm clock. The movie ends with the train pulling out slowly, with blasts of white steam, which may or may not symbolize tears. They shout goodbye to each other five times, wave sadly as the credits begin and the lights in the theater come on.

I like to think that Mathieu went home, brought down a bottle of wine, called up a guy friend, and tuned up his violin for a good cry, then called up some old girlfriends for the real fun.

My Clothes

My wife, as it happens, buys my clothes, and my daughter, it appears, picks them out. Today I'm wearing a bright yellow and black sweater with two balloon patches stitched to the front. It's comfortable, soft around the neck, and hangs just right on my body—and is an Ikeda design that people with money will recognize. I sort of like it, then again hate it. Yesterday when I went to Safeway and was standing in the check-out line, a baby with the ugliest drool on his fingers pointed and said, "Bubbles," meaning of course the printed balloons on the sweater.

I bought my groceries and returned home to put on a gray black checkered sweater, which I like a lot but unfortunately is out of style. It has also lost its shape and sags like an old mouth around the neck; a herd of fuzz balls has multiplied around the armpits. I've taken scissors to these herds, but they always come back, bigger and more numerous and greedy for more territory. I often have to pluck one or two of these fuzz balls from my hair-locked naval.

Wife and daughter. They have it out for me. Only last semester a student came up to me after class and asked if I had ever worked as a hair stylist. She said that I dressed like one, and even held my wrist like one, limp and crooked as the broken leg of a praying mantis. Her observation was strange, really surprising, because my image of myself was of a guy six feet tall, strong, and being strong, a little stupid about what a body can do, like break boards across a knee, and fall from a house and get up brushing dirt from a pair of Perry Ellis pants. I told my student, No, I had never worked as a hair stylist in Hollywood, and no, I wouldn't accept a late paper without knocking it down a grade.

Wife and daughter. They packed my shoulder bag when I went to Fresno with these dainty summer shorts and the cannery-yellow and lavender argyle socks that had my guy friends, all redneck Mexicans, laughing and spilling beer and sunflowers seeds. They blew kisses to me, and lifted their eyebrows at one another, as if to ask, has Gary jumped to the other side?

My family encourages me to wear an earring, which I do, and to carry a purse, which more and more men are doing—and not a woman's purse, but a manly and sophisticated burgundy tote by Tanino Crisci, which would go well with a Crombie overcoat. I've said no to the purse, but have considered the his-and-her robe by Christian Dior.

But I kind of like the clothes they buy me, because they're deceiving about what's really inside my head. Like the pink Geoffrey Beene Corduroy pants and the equally pink Enrico Coveri shirt with its sleeves that end at the elbows and puff into Japanese lanterns when I walk briskly. I like them, and like the Lorenzo Banfi belt and the Calvin Klein underwear. My clothes look cute, bright and cheerful, but the truth of the matter is that I'm not cute, bright or cheerful, but more on the mean side. I carry a knife, for instance, and a telescopic baton—the kind Korean police use—and am less than a year away from my black belt in Tae Kwon Do.

I don't believe in violence, though, partly because it's stupid and partly because I'm Catholic. I'm also fond of my Baker-Benjes shoes, which would crease with wrinkles should I have to kick someone very hard. I'm also fond of my face, seamless above the brow, thanks to my wife's hydrominerali skin revitalizing extract from Princess Marcella Borghese. If I were to get in a fight, I might risk soiling my clothes and this new look.

I think of myself, and I think of others. There's not enough wool in our skirts and suits to hide what's inside our heads, like greed and lust and your basic human wretchedness. But we try, nevertheless, and spend gobs of money on our image which is an outright lie. At this moment I'm at the business library in San Francisco. The man across from me is dressed in a corduroy jacket with patches on the elbows; he looks warm, polite, fatherly, the kind of father in fact who would encourage his children to jump in his lap to hear stories. But I would bet money that he's mean to his children and nasty to his wife, but thank God, a pushover in a fight. And this woman in a business suit appears competent as she works her Parker Brothers pen across a yellow pad. But I'd bet even more money that every third word is misspelled and she has no idea what she's doing in her job.

I let my wife and daughter have their little joke. They dress me like a doll and then let me act animal when I leave the house. How they love it.

Insomnia

A friend writes:

Every so often when I have slept poorly and am at a meeting with a tooth-nibbled yellow pencil, I will look up and to my astonishment see the people around me as pieces of talking meat. The jaws move up and down, and they have a moist sheen, like chicken breasts under clear plastic. I close my eyes, say to myself, "God, stop this," and when I open my eyes am so relieved that they're back to normal: men and women discussing ways to make money.

There's something wrong with me upstairs. I don't know what to do about this. My priest says that I should pray, which I've been doing. But I have a question I can't raise to Father Kieran. When I pray, I can only see the right side of God's face, and He's always kneeling at a rock. Is this how we're supposed to see God? God at a rock, in prayer?

I would like to ask my wife what she sees. I would like to ask my son about his bedtime prayers. Usually when I'm about to ask them, the other self inside me says, "Let's go for a walk." I will get up and walk, and sometimes close my eyes for a few steps—and there He is, God kneeling at his rock. One time a neighbor saw me walking with my eyes closed. I smiled, only slightly embarrassed, which amazed me because four or five years ago, I would have been haunted by shame to have someone see me walking with my eyes closed.

I read a lot to keep from thinking, see movies alone, and am eager to do the dishes three or four times a day, with the radio on. I like to take corners sharply when I drive, really hug the corners so that leaves and paper cups fly up. One time when an ice cream wrapper flew up on the hood, I made a bet with myself that I could drive a mile without it flying off. When it did, I laughed a lot and could hardly control the car.

I've written in my notebook, "I like to take corners sharply," and have studied the meaning of that sentence, tracing the words so that after half an hour nearly the whole page is pencilled black. I then lie down on the couch, with my arms at my side, and try to sleep.

Recently I have thought about how when my wife is happy with me, I go inside myself, look down, and without even closing my eyes see God at his rock. I don't like it when she does that, hugs me I mean, but will hug her back, make a lover's face and kiss. Once she lets go, my face slackens and I return to my usual malaise. I will go outside to the backyard and sit in a chair and think it's all right to count how many times the gold fish nibble air on the surface. I will take my cat in my lap and tenderly pull at her loose fur; I will let my son sit in my lap and tell me about his day; I will even say, "Come here, Barbara" to my wife. She will join me and sit on my lap, which only makes me nervous because I don't know what to do except to say things like, "In eight years the house will be paid off."

This past week I searched for people who look like me, look and eat their sandwiches slowly. They are all over, as close as the park across from my work, and their lunch is thin meat, an apple, milk drunk from a straw. They cross their legs, throw crumbs at thick-throated pigeons, and have a joyless look about them. So that's what I look like, I think. I watched a man in a blue suit crumble his paper bag, place it in his lap like a ball, and stare vacantly ahead, as if he were waiting for someone, a friend or lover. But no one came to visit him except waddling pigeons, which looked like a portion of the sea, blue and rolling, with a splash of white when they scattered skyward.

After lunch I crossed the street to St. Helen's, went in, and listened to the rosary, and was struck how the people in prayer were like pigeons in the park, mumbling and hunched into themselves. I lit a candle, stared at the flame that wavered left, then right, like a pendulum. I caught my head moving, however sightly, with the flame. I stopped its movement and returned to work and called up friends I had not heard from in a long time.

I think of a poet who said, "Remember the dying and you'll be all right." I'm going to remember this. I'm going to remember that God has a left side to his face too, and that the poor are ambassadors of good will. I have to stop my worry and sleep. It's too late for today, but tomorrow I'm going to wake, let my wife hug me, and try to open my eyes as wide as I can and remember that we only have one turn at living. And no more.

I Love My Students

I love my students. This spring semester I'm teaching poetry writing to a young woman from New York. Is she the only student in the class? No, but she's the one I look at mainly, mostly because she has this boy-girl look with freckles and a pixie haircut and just enough boobs to make her a girl. She also has a slight overbite, which is fascinating to me in the opposite sex. Some men enjoy tall scissoring legs, some breasts, some the fall and rise of a heart-shaped fanny. But for me it's an overbite that brings tears to my eyes.

Where does this fascination come from? I'm not certain, but I think it might be traced to Sue Zimm, a tomboy from the old street with a rabbit-face smile. When she wasn't beating me up, I liked her a lot, and almost fell in love with her when I had to unhook her bleeding leg from her father's twenty-five foot radio antenna on top of the house. She had climbed it on a $.25 bet, smiled her rabbit face at us boys on the ground, and was descending quite nicely when she slipped and her leg got caught (and lucky for her, or it might have been a head first flight all the way down) in one of the rings, falling backward so that she was hanging upside down. And it was a great day for her father. He had a chance to use his ham radio: he called the fire department, an ambulance, and a cousin of his, a photographer, to take pictures of Sue in a stretcher crying for her quarter.

My wife of eleven years, as it happens, is beautiful. She's also very smart, a good cook, a perfect lover, reasonably crazy, and fun to be with. But alas, she has no overbite, and if there's a flaw in our marriage it's this simple fact. I once mentioned this to her, and she said, "I'm sorry" and cried, or at least buried her face in the pillow and made noises. But since she now knows my preference for teeth, she often gets her way. She'll purse her lips, stick out her front teeth, and ask, "May I have a new jacket?" or "Can we go to the movies tonight?" My heart will rumble alive. "Yes," I'll say. "It's a great idea," I'll comment—and grow delirious with love and beg, "Can you keep your mouth like that when you eat popcorn?"

But back to my student, Wendy I will call her. She is smart and smartly dressed each class meeting and author of the line: Lavender is the favorite color of the gods. When I asked her how she knew this, she shrugged her shoulders and said that she had a hunch; she crossed her legs (which are not bad to look at) and asked if poetry writing isn't just a bunch of hunches with a title? I laughed and the class followed along, with Wendy finally joining in, her overbite revealing its glossy beauty that caused me to grow suddenly sad. I opened our poetry anthology and read poems about death. My students loved me for my melancholy.

Wendy knows that I like her. She thinks, however, it's because of her face, which is washed with clever light that is innocence itself, and her body, which is small and athletic. She also thinks that she has a keen personality, and a mind to go with it. What words would I use to explain my love for her overbite? How would I ask, please nibble here, and point to my neck. I can't think of any, so my love does not advance.

Wendy, and so many others, are full of life, cheerful, hopeful, and fun to hear talk. There are also students, though, with horrible lives: their parents are wife-beaters, alcoholics, indifferent and mean. And they themselves—the students—

have talked to me about abortions, God, roommates on expensive drugs, and mean boyfriends who scare them by doing wheelies on reckless motorcycles. Only last semester a very attractive student, with no overbite but years of orthodontic work, came to my office to explain her absence from class and the three late papers. She was very quiet and nervous, and sat down on the edge of a chair, not looking at me. When she raised her face, her eyes were moist. She said that her mother had died of cancer, and her family, father especially, who was also ill, was taking it very badly. I was caught off guard by this piece of news, and moved by her display of sorrow, because I had assumed that I would hear the typical story about being down with the flu or behind with other classes, or both. I played with my pencil, looked out the window and the white clouds stalled in the windless sky, and considered what I should say, what I should do. Am I not somewhat wise? I thought. In the end, I said I would overlook her absences (three weeks), she would write two more papers, and we would call it even.

I saw this student just a few days ago shopping in downtown Berkeley. I was surprised to see her, smiled, and asked how she was doing. She was applying to graduate school in architecture, was engaged and had just moved to a swanky apartment with a cousin. She then prodded me with a hand on my elbow over to the bench to introduce me to her mother. Something happy drained out of me; how could this be? We shook hands, exchanged some pleasantries, and parted, the student thinking, "He wasn't a bad teacher," and I, staggering down the street, thinking, "Her mother's come back to life? I've been used!"

This treacherous student, with perfect teeth, will go on to design buildings that will fall in time. She's no one to me. I love Wendy and Sue Zimm and my wife, especially when she purses her lips, as she did last week, and asks, "Do you like my new robe, or this?" She throws open the robe, and my eyes go crazy with her nakedness.

Good For Nothing

We're good at doing nothing, Jon and I, and once stood in a line to try to get a job with the telephone company. But the line was long, around the corner into the next century for all we knew. After two hours we were in the glass door, which was pawed greasy by men and women, and dogs who had trotted over to investigate the hub-hub. We licked our yellow pencils and filled out forms in triplicate. Finished, we rode our bikes back to my apartment, sat on the steps, and dreamed up ways to make money without doing too much, like teaching or the priesthood or wiggling our fannys at bachelorette parties.

The next week I was circumsized, and Jon was kind enough to ride his bike over with a bagful of apples on his knee. I was 23, just married, and brave I guess. I don't know why I did it, except that Dr. Taira, the westside saint whose patients were poor people, bargained, "I can do it for 75 bucks," when I had gone in to get a tetanus shot. I had always wanted to be circumsized and thought, "That's cheap."

Jon sat on the bed's edge and asked with a chaw of half-chewed apple in his mouth, "Does it hurt?" I drank from the water glass on the nightstand and said, "Only when I laugh." He then told me a joke about a man who was so absent-minded that he ate his dog, and when he was finished and picking his teeth a feeling of loneliness overwhelmed him. He went to his backyard and called, "Here, boy, come here." This made me laugh a little, but not enough to make that crown of stitches move in their holes.

It was too late for me to become a priest, I was married, and liked square meals and overhead lights, not candles. And I couldn't dance at bachelorette parties, because I was shy as a penguin with people I didn't know. I was also too young to teach. So I stayed home and every morning dusted the living-room, did the dishes, and herded our cat Benny's new litter of patchwork kittens from the house to the backyard. In the afternoon I rode my bike, with Jon at my side, in search of work. But it only depressed us. Everyone was riding bikes, with their mouths hanging open like sacks. The town was poor, and getting poorer because it was making thirty-nine babies a day—or so we read in the paper. This was the cause for worry.

At my apartment we sat on the steps and ate oranges, which were old and puckered like elbows because it was sum-mer, many months since they had been picked from the tree. "What do you want to do?" Jon asked. I flicked an orange peel at a kitten who jumped straight up in the air, half-scared and half-delighted by the peel. "I don't know, maybe we should do something." We stared straight ahead, a little empty in the head. I don't know where Jon went in his silence, but (God knows why) for a moment pictures of my sister in her Girl Scout dress filled my head. We snapped out of our funk thought, when we finished our oranges. We watched the cats watch us, and then got up to hose the suckers into hiding.

One day Jon rode up on his bike while I was hosing the cats from the porch. He had an interview to work at a mental hospital in Reedley. I was sad by this piece of news; it meant that he would work, put on flesh so that his ribs would never show again, and jumble coins in his pocket. His last job was as an assistant in a cancer lab at UC-Irvine, where we had gone to school, and he sort of made a mess of that one: when he was cleaning out a large jar, labeled *Research Important*, he allowed a salamander to wiggle from his grasp and slip down the drain. He looked down the drain, and the salamander looked up at him, wiggled his body, and disappeared forever.

He got the hospital job and went to work almost immediately. And immediately he faced his first problem: a young girl was walking around in the middle of summer with a snow jacket on. Jon knew what this meant. She had cut her wrists and was trying to hide them by wearing heavy clothing. Cool Jon, remembering the salamander with its pencil-dot eyes, got up slowly because he didn't want her to know that he knew. She would start running, lose a lot of blood, and maybe pale like a vampire. It would be all his fault, and once again he would have to get on his bike and ride around looking for work. No, he played it just right; he approached the girl and said, "Let me see." She let him see, and took off the jacket when he asked.

When Jon came over with his first pay check, I was eating oranges on the step. The kittens, now fat as water balloons, were licking themselves dry. Beads of water hung on their eyelashes. Jon told me to throw the orange away and that he was going to treat me to a hamburger, with the works. We crossed the street to Sir Pedaburger, ate like wild Romans, and returned to the apartment to lie under the orange tree and let the kittens jump up and down on us and play in our hair. They were frisky in their three-month lives, and we were lazy as old dogs in a hundred-degree heat. But when Carolyn, home from work, turned the hose on us, we jumped like the cats and picked up the nearest hoes and looked busy. We knew that although we were full, dinner was just around the corner, and if we expected to eat we had to pull our weight. We faced the scraggly garden. The cats faced us, their heads nodding *yes* as they followed the up and down motion of the hoe. We stopped to wipe our brows and cough from the dust.

We called them good-for-nothing fuzzballs, and they meowed at us to get to work.

Colors

If not an apple in one hand and desire in another, if not a novel and characters falling in and out of love, then something of that Saturday morning when you and I drove to Reedley, your hometown, where we walked its main street, hip to hip, my arm around your shoulder, your arm around my waist. We window-shopped, pointing at gleaming sale items. The 20% off toaster, the 30% off blender with ten speeds, the freight-damaged luggage at half off. We sat on a bench in a small park and watched sparrows, twig-brown, fly away with twigs and grass; one even flew away with a cotton ball. We wandered through a drug-store and stopped at the magazine rack. *Glamour* was a month old, dusty when you picked it up and thumbed a breeze in our faces, stopping at a page that was mostly words, not ads for clothes and perfumes and Cinderella shoes. You looked up and said, "My favorite color is red, red and black." I smiled the shallow smile of happiness, not paying attention to what you had just said, or why. Then I thought about it, and was baffled. It didn't follow or make sense. Why did you all of a sudden acquaint me with your favorite colors? Later, however, when I was back at my apartment and on my bed, exhausted from trying to keep up my end of the conversation, it would sink in as a truth: you were starting to tell me about yourself, little by little. First colors, then later movies and books and old boyfriends, one who was married and wouldn't leave you alone. The magazine in your hand was a thing to hold as you talked.

I had done the same. Outside on the street I mentioned that my favorite color was forest green and, your hand tightening around my waist, you asked, "What color is that?" I tried to describe it by saying that it was a color like a large forest seen close up. That didn't seem clear. I said it was like a tree with moss or maybe just the moss itself, and said that it was one of the colors in the 64 Crayola box. We left Main Street and walked aimlessly through the residential streets, where a dirty dog poked his wet nose around your knees and tried to go higher. I told you how when I was in the 3rd grade Sister Marie made the class break their crayons in halves. She said that we could color better that way, and that Van Gogh, Monet, and Whistler worked with crumbs and silver-thin pastels. We could do the same, Sister Marie reasoned, and make pretty art like the masters. Some of the girls cried as they broke their crayons, and I didn't feel great about it either because it was my first 64 Crayola.

We had walked from town to the river where we stared at the water, its surface full of autumn clouds and the branches of the cottonwoods. I became quiet and transfixed by the movement of the river. My brother came to my mind, how he used to rock-jump at Piedra to see who would fall first. I laughed to myself and told you that I was thinking of my brother. You didn't say anything. You watched my eyes, which were so young that they didn't know what to settle on, you or the water and the image of my brother inside my head. I talked about Rick, poor artist, and about myself and how when I was young I thought of becoming an oceanographer but now knew I was lousy at math and wasn't math something you needed to study the sea? I talked nonsense until I ran out. When you leaned against me, I took two steps back and leaned against the rock. I brought you into my arms, kissed, moved my hands up and around. I took your hand and led you into some brush where we kissed more, lay on wet grass, pulled at each other until our clothes were off and I was in you, both of us making hurt noises. When I pulled away I was amazed that you were so pink, pink against black, which was almost like your favorite colors, and that where we lay in the brush was like my favorite color, forest green. I took a leaf from your hair, two tangled in your sweater, but put them back when I lay with you again.

Fire

The fire is now dead, the color of an old Dickens tramp. Earlier it was red hot, sucking life from rain-green boards, egg cartons, wadded newspapers, and a log from a woodpile on the side of the house. I tossed the log in and listened to the snails, attached to its rough side, hiss their watery deaths. I watched the small teeth of flames eat until there was nothing left except embers that blinked and popped when wind swirled from the chimney.

I like fires. I like to light candles at birthday parties, light them not once but twice because there is something beautifully grotesque in candles melting down to their stubby ends. I like to set the dusty black coals on the barbecue, drench them with lighter fluid, and be the one to toss in a match: the fire bursts and my face shines like the crazed penny. If the chicken is oily, so the better. Its grease drips onto the coals and flames shoot up between the grill, like the hands of prisoners. I flick water on the flames; the coals hiss and steam and finally after hours in the dark, while we are inside and in bed, cool to gray dust under their larger cousins, the stars.

In San Francisco the bay is pleasant to watch, either from an apartment-building rooftop or close up. The sailboats dip and rise on the water; wind surfers skim over white-tipped waves which are pulled along by the wind and the moon's gravity toward the rocky beach. Children play in the sand, dogs frolic idiotically at the water's edge, and lovers fly kites or walk along, hip and hip, teasing the waves. But after a minute or so, the spectacle of the bay dulls to monotony: you look around and wish the hell you were elsewhere.

The picturesque bay is a tranquil moment, a house on fire is a wicked occasion. It makes us stop, look up in inspired awe, become so mesmerized by the fire that an officer could tell you move back and you would not hear him. Your stare locks on the crumbling porch, a door wreathed in flames, or maybe the roof with its aura of hot sparks shooting skyward.

When I was a kid of four or five I tried to burn down our house, but (thank God) only managed to singe the back porch. This was my first disappointment in life, my inability to create excitement for the neighbor kids who egged me on to get the fire going. My mother singed me with a good beating, and chased my brother around the house with a heated fork.

Sometimes even now I will stop to stare at a leaf-fire in the gutter, just stare at the fiery tongues until my eyes water with smoke. More often than not, it's a kid who started that fire; started it but left because someone called him away, leaving me—and the kid inside my soul—to stare until an appointment calls me away.

Kids and fire. Christmas is around the corner. A book of matches would be as pleasing as a bright toy—and cheaper. But of course I could not offer such a gift, say to my daughter or nephew, "Merry Christmas, here's a box of wooden matches." We're not allowed to do this. But I would love to slip my nephew two or three matches and tell him to enjoy himself but not to get carried away. "Burn some leaves," I would suggest, "but leave my car alone."

Sometimes while driving I-5 in the Valley I will spot smoke on the horizon—control burning of the spent fields, a house on fire, a crazy with a zippo lighter and a lot of card-board? A genie of smoke climbs slowly skyward, and I can't help but think, what is the message? I've noticed that smoke doesn't go up randomly, but is circular, a clock-wise motion, a thick-to-thin action, and high enough for all to see. Didn't Indians scan the horizon with one hand shading their brow? Didn't Greek Gods send down smoke and lightning to scare the hell out of man? Didn't the priest burn incenses so that our eyes would fill with tears? Often I will try to *read* the smoke, take a stab at our fate, and come up with notions of wealth and contentment and long illustrious lives. My wife, who'll be reading her beauty magazine as I drive, will not even look up. She thinks I'm a little crazy. She'll say, "Yes, that's a possibility," and turn the page.

My fascination has nothing to do with pyromania. I am not an arsonist, or a person to jump up and down in delight when a hotel catches fire. Freud might write on his pad, "Sexual energy and the unconscious." He can write what he pleases, but I think of fire as an instinct toward destruction, which is both good and bad. Fire is savage, a reminder of evil which both repels and attracts us, and a hint of what is to come, provided that there is a hell for the wicked to leap through without rest.

So I have my little savagery. The fire is now dead, cold as a stone, but earlier it was hot as the first planetary flames. On this autumn day I sat with a coffee and stared and stared, and thought nothing in particular. I could have thought of lovers, a good fight with someone on the street, money and its finger-stink of evilness. But I just sat on the couch, trans-fixed by the flames that leapt and fell and leapt again. "Fa-ther," I could have said, "father, father"—for that is what it is. Prometheus gave us fire, warmth for the body and soul, and now clings to his rock, as we in turn give warmth to our children and in time will cling to our rock with no one to hear our small agonies.

Reprobate

Once I wanted to fool with this woman who wasn't my wife but a neighbor, ten years younger, and green in the way that I was ragged red. She wasn't terrific looking, a little pointed in the face like a bird, only reasonably smart, only reasonably fine in body, but pleasant, and kind, and very, very Catholic, which ended about everything that I had in mind, except coffee and donuts and some Christian music we listened to on the tape deck in her car.

"The Lord is with us always," she said.

"I think so too," I said flatly, not wanting to get her started. We listened to folk music, stuff with the same message song after song, and ate donuts and got as comfortable as we could in her Datsun. But I soon grew bored. I thought, what the heck, maybe we should argue. So I said, "Don't you think God sometimes takes us for granted?" My friend, shocked awake with donut crumbs falling from her mouth, turned up the music and yelled at me with a great, moist force that fogged the window.

One night I wanted to fool with a woman who had been around—lovers as numerous as spent leaves on the ground—and utterly used by men who needed late night rides because their cars were broken down. She was good with her sadness, knew how to talk and wet her lips without being crude, knew Spain and Italy, but was bad song lyrics when she started talking about her boyfriends, those leaves on the ground stirred back to life. I drank my beer and listened, as she sucked on her cigarette and blew out her story:

Hank was nice, but wore motorcycle boots that sometimes kicked me. Bobby was OK, but Bobby's friend Charles was better, except he was married and had problems with his ole' lady. I didn't see anyone for a while, except for William and he was a roofer who had a pretty good job and was nice even if he smelled like tar. He used to bring me watermelons from Chowchilla; his Daddy had a farm there, and dogs. I like dogs, especially Ray's, he was the first black guy I did it with. He was really sweet, except his girlfriend was a pushy bitch, never gave him slack or love from what he told me.

I drank my beer, got drunk, and in the end, two in the morning, got up to pee and went right to bed, alone.

But I liked her, bad song and all, and I also liked a girl who was almost a woman, seventeen or so, extremely bright with quick eyes and a smile like something coming on. She was a waitress at a favorite Chinese restaurant, and though I never asked her name, I assumed it was Sue. The Sue I knew when I was a boy had an overbite that was deliciously erotic and fun to bump against when we kissed. My waitress smiled an overbite; smiled as she hurried to clear tables, pick up bills, make change, refill water glasses and teapots. When she would take my order, I would be deliberately slow and full of questions. What is Paradise Pork? Slow Boat Prawns? And this, here, Family Happiness on Rice? As she explained each dish, I stared openly at her teeth and a longing so deep, so confusing rose to my cheeks and stayed there. Bending over to look at my menu, she sucked her pencil and said, "This is good, and this too if you like it spicy." In the end, I always chose my favorite, Wonderful Flavored Chicken, and chose not to make a fool out of myself by asking her out. And if I had, what would I say? What would we do? Go to a movie, hold hands? Would I beg her to couple her teeth with mine and give myself up to the police the next day for fooling with a minor—not before of course telling her her overbite is like no other? If Freud were alive, he would have new territory to work with.

It's the old punishment, love on the way down. I'm 34, still thin, still not bad to look at, and wanting more from my wife and others. I think of women, talk to women, and studiously follow the lingerie ads in my wife's *Vogue*. Today I'm going to 12:05 mass at Old St. Mary's, and I'm going to pray for my poet friends that they may heal themselves in their own way, and the poor that they may eat, but mostly I'll pray for myself that I may stop my dreaming. I'll pray, but also look around. Yesterday there was a woman in front, third pew to the left, near the statue of St. Joseph, and she was more beautiful than plain, in an overcoat that snapped when she walked up to take communion. She was tall with short hair, and strong enough to meet my grip in a handshake. Strong. Strong enough to break limbs from trees and chase me around when I misbehave. This is still another beauty I find in women.

Guess Work

A little wind can rake the sky of its yellowy balm. It can do the same to the mind. In this autumn weather I think of the young woman I saw on campus today sitting on a grassy knoll with her gathered skirt pinched between her knees. She finished a sandwich and flipped pages of a notebook back and forth. A row of conjugated French verbs? Dates from American history? Math formulas that resemble eye charts? I wasn't certain. I watched her longingly, though, because there was beauty in her face and in her sophomore worry. Was it all necessary, her intense study for a pop quiz on plankton or the Dead Sea? Surely professors would not demand such stuff.

I know little about this woman. But there are clues. She was small, Japanese perhaps, and smartly dressed, which means she either had a summer job or is the only daughter from a good family, perhaps a 200 acre farmer from the San Joaquin Valley. I believe it's the latter. Her arms were dark. She probably helped in the packing house or handled a dusty Dodge truck that ran errands for her father, a gruff Nisei in khaki, who walked in his orchard that was weighed down with ripe apricots and Mexicans on unsteady ladders. I could have been one of them, a worker that is, but woke up in high school to see that I didn't want to stand on a ladder with buckets tied to my hip and babies screaming in my ear when I got home. I ain't gonna do field work, I thought, and went to college, sat on campus grass among other ambitious Mexicans, conjugated English verbs, read history, and worried over the up-and-down graphs in geology that showed the country falling into the sea, in 10,000 years.

But I'm here. This young woman is on my mind. Her dress was deep red, as I remember, and her shoes, the kind of pumps my wife wears, were off her feet and set like twin lamps in front of her. They were noticeably new, not yet scuffed or rain-warped or sagging. The fall semester was a week old. She had yet to walk places, say hello to new people, and, like so many others, take a boyfriend with whom she would pet heavily in a parked car. On Saturday mornings they would drink coffee and hold hands through football games. By the time their love ends, her shoes will be a clunk in the closet, and little else.

But who knows, maybe I'm wrong. Perhaps she's the daughter of a pharmacist, not a farmer, and she wasn't studying for history or biology but doing a crossword puzzle because she was bored with school. She doesn't like her classes, and thinks her professors are dolts and the campus men just boys who want to escort her to football games. She told one who kept reminding her he was pre-med that she didn't work as an "escort" and found football just dumber than checkers.

Maybe she's neither the daughter of a farmer nor a pharmacist but of a vice-president of a large bank in New York City, and she's a practicing Buddhist who lived her childhood in a Jewish neighborhood where everyone tipped his hat and was friendly. That's it. She's from New York, three time zones from home, which now explains her sadness to me, but doesn't explain the letter she received earlier in the week from home informing her the family dog died. That made her very sad, as did the B– on the mid-term in biology.

It's guesswork. It's what I'm best at when the wind comes and the coin-bright sun rides above the immobile trees. It's a trade with absolutely no market. I can sit on a bench, clear-headed and curious about the world, and start a life without so much as getting up. Women come and go. Their skirts flair and bounce beautifully when they hurry to class or coffee or weekend affairs. They're young and hopeful. My hope is that the lines around my mouth don't deepen too much, now that I'm thirty-four and getting older. From a distance, when you look upon others who have no idea how awful it feels, anything is possible.

This Man

My father died in an accident, and it was no accident that the man who fell on him and broke my father's neck never again came to our house, though he was a friend of the family who lived only five houses away. He was that person who walked past our house every day on his way to Charlie's Grocery for meat, a head of lettuce, milk for his children. After our father's death he took a different route; he chose instead Sarah Street to get to the grocery.

I wonder how it was for him, what he felt. Nearly thirty years later I can see him in my mind. He's on the couch, tired from the work of candling eggs for Safeway, his boots off and shirt open; or it's summer, hot, and he's in the back yard staring transfixed at the water running from a hose into the garden. I see his wife shout from the kitchen that she needs butter. He gets up slowly and laces up his boots; he turns away from the river of water, already drying between the rows of squash and tomato plants, and coils the hose. He takes the quarter from his wife and, starting off to the store, thinks of Manuel, our father, maybe sees his face whole, maybe sees his face twisted and on the ground, the blood already drying like the water in the garden. But how much? How much of our father was on his mind? Did the kids in the street distract him, the neighbors on porches, a barking dog? Did he sing inside his head, worry about bills, maybe think of work and the eggs that travelled endlessly on the conveyor? He bought his butter, went home to eat with his children, who after the accident never came over to play with us. We waved to them when we walked passed their yard and, behind their fence, they waved back.

Shortly after the accident we moved away from our south Fresno neighborhood, and he and his family became those names we never said in our house. Something happened in our family without us being aware, a quiet between mother and children settled on us like dust. We went to school, ate, watched television that wasn't funny, and because mother never said anything, father, too, became that name we never said in our house. His grave was something we saw in photographs; his remembrance those clothes hanging in the back of the closet.

I remembered this man from the old street when I saw him years later buying cigarettes at a gas station. I was filling the tires on my bike. His car was large, and he himself was large, his girth like a tree: I like to think he was eating for two, himself and father, who was inside like a worm taking his share; that after all those years he still thought of Manuel and the afternoon when he climbed that ladder with a tray of nails on his shoulder, lost his balance, and fell. This is my hope, for my sake and this man's, because we should remember the dead, call them back in memory to feel their worth.

He must have felt guilt and shame, or otherwise he would have walked up our street to the grocery or said more than "Hi" to me at the gas station. But it's not guilt or shame that I want to feel for him but sadness, that a man like so many others is dead and the photographs we own do no good in assembling Father once again into flesh and bone. We lived poor years because he died. We suffered quietly and hurt even today. Shouldn't this mean something to him?

Sadness not guilt. I have felt both. As a kid I often thought about the sea, yearned for the sea, and imagined that where I lived was the wrong place; that being poor and Mexican was wrong. During those years I thought of the sea a lot, not of Father, and am ashamed of this. It's so strange to me now: I had maps of the sea, books, model ships I set proudly on doilies for visitors to notice. I had questions for teachers— How big was Atlantis? Did the Vikings really discover America? Are Eskimos Chinese who live in the cold? This went on for years, my fascination with the sea, and for years I never dared mention my father to my mother or my sister and brother. He was gone, and we were here, and the man who did this to us was nowhere to be found.

It would take a doctor to explain our loss, or a wise man to sit me down and quiet my nervous knee that I can't stop. It's strange; my brother has the same tick. When we meet for Thanksgiving, his knee, like mine, jumps up and down. It won't stop. When I ask, "What's wrong," he says, with his arms folded behind his head, "Nothing. Nothing at all."

Piedra

The river was gray-blue when you sat on the bank, and gray when you stood on the bank, and swift and cold no matter how you looked at it in autumn. River rock splayed the water, so that it leaped white like fish; leaped up and fell back to join the gray-cold current, southward, to feed Avocado Lake.

Piedra. River of rock, place where our family went for a Saturday picnic. It was a fifteen-mile drive past plum and almond orchards, dairies, the town with its green sign, Minkler—Population 35, *Mexicanos* pruning orange trees on ladders, and our mother's talk that if our grades didn't improve we would be like *those* people. Past cows with grassy jaws, past fallen fences, groceries, tractors itching with rust, the Griffin ranch with its mowed pasture and white fence that proclaimed he was a gentleman farmer. We gawked at his ranch, and counted his cows, which seemed cleaner, better looking than the fly-specked ones we had passed earlier.

I dreamed about Griffin's daughters. I imagined that their hair was tied in ponytails and bounced crazily when they rode horses in knee-high grass near the river. They were the stuff of romance novels, sad and lonely girls who were in love with the stable boy, who was also sad and lonely but too poor for the father's liking, because he himself had once been poor but now was rich and liked to whip horses, cuss, and chase gasping foxes at daybreak.

My dreaming stopped when the road narrowed, gravel ticked under a fender, and we began our climb through the foot-hills. I was scared that our stepfather would forget to turn the wheel and we would roll slowly off the cliff into the brush and flint-sharp boulders. But he always remembered in time to turn and weave the car, its tires squalling through the hills that were covered with grass and oak trees. Then—just like that—around a bend the river came into view and our ears were filled with the roar of water.

Like so many other parents, ours didn't know what to do with themselves while we played. They would gaze at the river from our picnic table, drink coffee from thermoses, keep up one-word conversations, and smoke cigarettes. They looked tired. I felt sorry for them, but not sorry enough to keep them company. I joined my brother and sister in a game of hide-and-seek in the brush that ran along the river; played hide-and-seek until it turned into a game of army that would turn into a game of nothing at all. We would just sit in the brush and overturn rocks to see what they hid. They hid glittery sand and soggy leaves, smaller rocks, bottle caps, and toads and lizards that scared us so that we let out sharp screams when they ran along our fingers. We played games that we could have played at home, but it seemed so special to be there, the river loud at our side, the fishermen shushing us, dogs knee-deep in water and drinking.

When we were called back, it was for a lunch of hot dogs and barbecue chips and soda, and then back to playing. One time, however, I didn't join my brother and sister, but went on my own to hike toward a mountain that mother said would take a long time to climb. I told her I could do it in twenty minutes. She drank coffee from the thermo's cup. She didn't seem to hear me. I started off, leaving my brother and sister to call me names because I didn't want to go with them to the dam to throw rocks.

The mountain seemed so close I could touch it. I walked

forever, as a kid would say, and climbed a barbed-wire fence that said No Trespassing, and continued on until I was out of breath. I stopped, looked back, and was surprised at how far I had come. The picnic table was far below, my parents just shadows on the benches. The river was thin as a wrist, and even Friant dam seemed smaller now that the gushing water spilled noiselessly from its opened valves. I liked where I was. The wind was in my hair, the sun in the yellow grass. I sat down, hugging my knees, and scanned the hills, which were brown and tree-specked and a purplish dark where the sun did not reach; scanned the road for the roadside grocery where we had stopped to buy sodas. Except for the wind it was quiet, and I was quiet too, with just one thought, and this thought was happiness. I was happy. All the badness in my life was momentarily gone, flooded with sunlight, and I believed I could lie down in the grass *forever*. I will have my chance.

Cruel Friends

My friend Chris to me: "Soto, you're the only guy I know who can fit his dick inside a straw," which he said after I exaggerated what it could do. I laughed, lifted my beer but didn't drink, and maybe or maybe not said something, but if I did it was probably a feeble, "You fat punk."

But I had my day. Chris is a poet, and when he complained long distance over the phone how his work had just come back from *Poetry*, a magazine that my stuff frequently appears in, I said, "You know the secret, don't you?" Chris, becoming suddenly serious and quiet over the line, fell into my palm and asked, "No, what is it?" I paused for a long time, since it was *his* call and *his* money, not mine, before I said, "You got to send them good poems."

Chris and I once tacked a fellow poet's poetry collection onto a wall, laughed, and threw mean glares. Flies settled on the book, a moth beat against it for whatever light it could give, and within days the pages were yellow and dripping from the pull of gravity. We were nasty, and foul as the air inside a sponge. "The darkness that is," Chris mimicked in a poetic voice, one hand on a beer bottle, the other gagging his throat in disgust.

My wife tells me that women are not cruel to their women friends. But I've heard my sister say over the phone, "That pushy bitch," referring to a close friend. I've heard her gossip, throw names around like pies, shout, cuss, and bite a mean lip—and all on my phone, not even in the privacy of her own conscience.

But that's my sister, and she is different from most women, or is she? I've always imagined that most women were like my wife, sweet or reasonably sweet, rational, the better half of the world, those who keep us men from killing each other. But maybe not. Maybe they're as snide as we are. This is my problem, and my hope. I don't know how to see women, mainly because I'm a romantic who assumes that they are full of kindness and love, beauty and grace, and civility. The picture inside my head is this: I see my wife and her best friend having lunch, something light like a sandwich or a salad, or both if they have missed breakfast. Carolyn is talking about a pair of red and black gloves that were fifty percent off, and her friend, clearing her throat with a sip of iced tea with no sugar, responds with an exhuberant "Great." Her friend, salad fork poised, tells Carolyn that she would have bought this suit, except that she's saving her money for Christmas, that she wants to buy something special for her husband. Carolyn responds, "How lovely!" and bites into a sandwich.

No biting words, no meanness, no sleeze. Garbage doesn't fall out of their mouths, and if occasionally they talk dirt it's tidy, wrapped in paper, and not too stinky. With men, well, when the mouth opens, it's fuck this and fuck that, and swig of a cold beer.

Only recently, when my daughter, age eight, and I were shopping for a gift for her mother, I suggested a blouse that was—literally and unfortunately—straight-laced. My daughter, holding it up, said, "Come on, Dad, get with it. Meaningless designs are in." I have to wonder about myself, and my friends, most of whom are poets, poor and admittedly not well in the head, that if I can't pick out a gift for a woman, something easy like a Valentine card or flower for an anniversary instead of the functional drafting lamps and screwdriver kits I usually carry home—that if I can't choose something recognizably sweet and true to the occasion, how can I answer the more involved question about friendship? I've drunk my limit of coffee for today and I haven't waked up enough to muscle an idea from my head about women and friends.

On this subject, I have no idea what I'm talking about.

The Occasional Movie Reviewer, Part Two

After doing the laundry, some letter writing, some breakfast dishes, I decided to approach my wife, who was doing editorial work at the dining table, and ask if she wanted to see a matinee. I had in mind *Blue Velvet*, now playing at the Lumiere, which was only seven blocks away. She was only too glad to put aside her work and put on a coat. Instead of taking the cable car, we decided to walk all uphill, one hard step at a time, until we got to Mason where the Fairmont and the Mark Hopkins sit. The street leveled off. We began to enjoy the walk, and then suddenly, almost unexpectedly, the street began to point down, steeply, and we began to hurry along out of control, gravity doing its trick on us. Carolyn let go of my hand, as if to say, "Every person for herself." I looked at her. She was laughing, her hair like Van Gogh's "Cypresses," and pointing at a dog, almost out of control as he passed us, his eyes tearing from the onrush of wind and his tiny legs blurring like fans.

But soon the street leveled off and we were in front of the Lumiere, a few minutes late. Still, I had to have a candy bar, and while Carolyn went in to find seats, I crossed the street to the liquor store to buy a Milky Way. I returned to the theater in a hurry to discover that the movie had already started and the screen was flashing a close-up of an ear, presumably cut off, resting in weeds. There was an ant circling the ear rim, no, there were two ants, one having emerged from a dark recess. This is a weird one already, I thought, and bumped along the walls in search of Carolyn, my eyes still not used to the dark. I stepped on a toe, patted someone's head, and brushed against someone's bottom. Unable to find her, I sat down alone near the front. I wanted to see the movie and find out how the ear got there, and why.

These were the same questions the young man who had found the ear was asking. He had gone to the police, who concurred, with a dead-pan humor, that it was indeed a human ear and that something was up. They didn't know what, but they would certainly go to find out. With the help of a police detective's daughter, the young man, Jeffrey, decides to find out by breaking into Dorothy Vallen's apartment. How did he know that the police detective's daughter knew Dorothy was a prime suspect? Her room is above her father's office, and one evening while she was doing some homework, she had overheard a terrible conversation about people disappearing and heard the name Dorothy Vallens. This set her thinking about the world and her impermanence.

But I should stop now because it occurs to me that I have not set the scenario well enough to allow you to fully understand the meaning of the movie, since I arrived at the theater after the movie started and was baffled from the beginning, especially by the ear and those two ants. Let me help you by telling what I know. The movie takes place in a small town, with tree-lined streets and a polite, disease-free populace. Jeffrey is in his early twenties, and is good looking, wholesome, and morally correct. The detective's daughter, whose name I've already forgotten but for the sake of brevity I will call Babs, is seventeen, a high school student, and good looking, though often her mouth works into the shape of a slack lasso when she cries or smiles. She is blond, pretty, slim in the waist and cautious, being a detective's daughter and the sweetheart of a high school jock. And how did Barbara and

92

Jeffrey ever get to know each other? Well, she walked right out of the shadows on a dark night and said, "Are you the guy who found the ear? It has to do with Dorothy Vallens." At the time I thought this was a smooth transition, but now that I have had time to reflect, I think it was too easy a way of bringing together two people to share a common interest: I'm speaking of course of the ear and the two ants.

Now back to the review. Jeffrey and Babs, who is somewhat reluctant to get involved, work out their conspiratorial talk of getting into Dorothy's apartment at a low-life diner called the Abilene. Jeffrey bites into a french fry and explains his plan. He's going to pose as a pest control man, and while he's busy spraying the kitchen, she (Babs) is going to knock at the door and pester Dorothy with Jehovah's Witness material, thus giving him time to unlatch a window so that later he can break in and snoop about. At first she's reluctant, and makes her mouth like a lasso, saying that she has a date with her boyfriend and, well, she doesn't want to get involved. But in the end, she cooperates, mainly because she's finding Jeffrey more and more attractive, and what wouldn't she do for her man? So the next day he slips into workman's garb, shrugs a canister of insecticide onto his shoulder, and proceeds to climb seven flights and face Dorothy Vallens, who has pouting lips, a frightened look in her eyes, and ratted hair. Her apartment is creepy, with poor lighting and an oily-looking shag rug.

Better than unlatching a window, Jeffrey steals a set of keys, and the next night he breaks into her apartment, but not before taking in a show (with Babs, whose mouth is busy making lasso shapes) featuring Dorothy Vallens, better known at the night club as The Blue Lady. She starts off singing, in a Swedish lisp, "Blue Velvet." Prior to this I was unsure of whether I was seeing the movie *Blue Velvet* or had walked into the wrong theater, which would explain why I couldn't find Carolyn. The movie's title and the movie itself were not coming together to make a whole lot of sense, and nowhere in the movie was the color blue significant to the drama. I would have called it, *The Lost Ear*, *Jeffrey's Cause*, or maybe *Bad People in a Good Town*.

Anyhow, Jeffrey sneaks into Dorothy's apartment and is snooping in the dark when he hears a key being placed noisily in the lock. Startled, Jeffrey jumps into a closet from where he watches a sad downcast Dorothy enter the apartment, toss a purse on the couch, undress down to her bra and panties, and kiss what looks like a picture she has hidden under the couch. Jeffrey makes the mistake of knocking something over in the closet, which prompts a knife-wielding Dorothy to throw open the closet door, scare him by nicking his cheek and, having a change of heart, show her affection by pulling down his underwear (she's made him undress) and taking him into her mouth. This all stops when a rude knocking sounds at the door. Dorothy looks at Jeffrey, and Jeffrey looks at his penis. We are then introduced to Frank, who is loud and full of horrible language. He shouts for his drink, calls her names, rages, then asks Dorothy to sit on a chair, spread-legged and face turned away from him. He gets on his knees, cries, calls "Mommie, mommie"—and then slaps Dorothy and shouts, "Don't look at me!" He places a mask, the kind dentists use to make you go to sleep, over his nose and mouth and breathes deeply, very rapidly. Then, fully dressed, he humps her viciously, all the while calling her ugly names, and tender ones too, like "Mommie, Mommie," and screaming "Don't look at me!" Finished, he slaps her and leaves. This man has problems.

Jeffrey, who had in the meanwhile returned to the closet, comes out to comfort Dorothy, but she shrugs his hand away and instead asks him to beat her. Jeffrey, a nice boy really, obliges. He ends up going to bed with her and slapping her around because she wants it very badly, though I suspect he doesn't like it very much.

94

The movie is ugly. We see Dorothy humped again by Frank (with the ever present mask over his face) and later by a turned-on Jeffrey who feels it's his duty to comfort her and do what she asks. We see Jeffrey beaten up by Frank, while a fat go-go girl dances on a car roof. We see a homosexual with a strong left hook punch Jeffrey. We see drug money exchanged and a dead body hang from a window. We see Dorothy walking around the town naked, bruised and bloody from a bout with Frank. We see Frank on top of a body, performing sex I guess, and screaming, "Don't look at me!" We see Babs cry on her mother's shoulder and ask, "What's going on?", which was my question now that my Milky Way was gone. We see a corrupt cop so stiff in his death (he's been shot in the head) that he can't fall over, and instead is standing up, eyes open and staring his dead stare at another dead person bound and gagged but sitting in a chair with a long sock in his mouth. We see the townspeople still buying paint and hammers and believing in the future. We see Jeffrey, who has taken his place back in Dorothy's closet, shoot Frank in the forehead, and Babs' father, the detective who up until now hasn't done a thing, rush into the apartment, gun raised, then gun relaxed, as he turns to Jeffrey and says, "I guess that'll show them," referring to the dead bodies in the room. And finally we see Jeffrey and Babs embrace in the hallway and make out very heavily, as her father, a few feet away and oblivious that his daughter is being felt up by a young man who moments before had killed a very wicked man, points to the officers and the people from the morgue to carry off the bodies.

The movie ended with the larger question never being answered. Just whose ear was that? Why did any of this happen? Just what was Frank's problem? I went outside and waited for Carolyn, who came out minutes later with one hand in front of her face and blinking in the harsh light.

"Where were you?" I asked. She told me she was up

front, and that it was an ugly movie and that I had wasted her time. We trudged up the hill and then raced out of control downhill to our apartment where she returned to her editorial work—or tried to return because I had suddenly become romantic and was beckoning her to the couch with all the charm tactics I could muster. When I got no action, I went to the kitchen, searched for a clear plastic cup, and returned to the livingroom, snorting and breathing like Frank and whispering a crazed whisper, "Psycho drama, baby—and don't look at me!" She jumped out of her chair, butted my forehead with an open palm, and told me to go sit back down, that Mommie was coming soon but not now.

Blue Velvet is a movie I recommend if there's nothing else to do.

Happy

I'm a boy, aged five, and waiting for Lupita, Mom's friend, to come and take us away for the evening. I don't want to go because everything is so dirty at her house. My sister, a year younger, is with me, thumb in her mouth and rocking on the back porch. She's not happy that Mom has gone dancing for the evening. Neither of us says a word, though. We watch the ants crowd onto a watermelon rind that's sitting on the barbecue.

Finally Lupita's banged-up station wagon drives up. Although neither of us wants to go, we sigh and get up dusting off our bottoms.

"How are you, kids?" she asks.

"Fine," we both say without looking at her.

We climb in the back seat. A vinegary stench replaces the good air in our nostrils. Donald and Lloyd, about our age, are there, necklaces of dirt around their throats, their T-shirts like slaughterhouse aprons stained with peaches, bean juice, hotdogs they rolled clean when they fell in the dirt. Oh God, I think, it's going to be awful sleeping at their house. It's happening right there in the back seat. Donald and Lloyd are jumping up and down and singing. Are they happy? Yes, they are happy. Both of them are jumping in tubs of chow mein. Each time their feet come down there's the sound of snails being pulled apart. Jump, snail death. Jump, snail death. Lupita, mother of seven more on the way, pulls away from the curb. The baby in her lap is helping her steer. "Good driving," she says as the baby, wet fingers on the wheel, manages a tight corner. Lupita's laughter erupts like a chicken thrown from a speeding car. She weaves over the yellow line, laughs. She stops at a stoplight, laughs. A man on a bike is the funniest thing in the world, laugh, laugh.

I can't get it out of my mind. I keep thinking that the chow mein Donald and Lloyd are jumping on is dinner. I want to ask Lupita, "What are you gonna feed us?" but I'm too scared that she'll say chow mein. So I just hold on to the seat and close my eyes. The baby is hysterical with laughter at each corner when the car screeches and nearly turns over.

When we pull into the yard the oldest brother, Andy, is hanging from a telephone wire. His face is washed over with fear that he's going to fall.

"Very, very good," Lupita says to her baby. She takes the baby's hands and claps them together. Lupita looks up at Andy who's still readjusting his grip. "Look at my son. He's such a knuckle-head!"

We all get out of the car, and other sons and a daughter hop in to make up a game about going to hell to see who's there, but not before Donald and Lloyd carry in the chow mein, their feet shiny from the wetness. Now I know we're having it for dinner. Debbie looks at me and starts crying and sucks her thumb, making smacking sounds not so unlike chow mein being jumped on. Lupita takes her hand and says, "What's wrong? C'mon, be happy"—and pulls her inside the house where Marilyn, who's in my class at St. John's, is with a neighbor kid, Alfonso, and they're playing a game of bowling. They have one real pin, and the other pins are plastic detergent bottles. The bowling ball is real, with milky swirls and three holes in it. They can't pick it up or stop it, so once it goes it goes. The baby who was in Lupita's arms is yelling, "Bubble, bubble" at the ball. Her fingers are wet with drool.

She is happy. She races after the ball, which is bouncing off the walls in the hallway. Debra and I run out of the house before the baby, smashed to the floor, gets her air back to start crying.

Andy must have fallen because he's no longer hanging from the telephone pole. The kids who had jumped in the car are still in the car because hell is far away. One of them asks us to get in and come along. I shake my head no. He calls me a baby, spoil sport, and names in Spanish. Debra and I watch them for a while, and so does Lupita. She has come out with the bowled-over baby who has stopped crying. I can see, though, that her shoulders are still jerking with sobs.

"What characters," she says. "I wish they'd behave." She laughs, buries a farting kiss in her baby's neck, and walks over to her flowerbed and its one rose bush, which is more of a stick with three leaves than a live plant. She puts the baby down and begins to pinch off the aphids.

I don't like any of this, I'm thinking. Is this really fun? Do you have to be poor to be happy, because this family is so poor that beggars would give them money. I return inside. Arnold, the oldest, is at the kitchen stove. He asks, "Do you want to see a carnival?" I don't know what to say except, "I guess." With a pencil he stirs a pot. He then picks me up so that I can look in. There are things going around and around in there. When I ask him what they are, he says that they are pigeons. "See the heads?" Knuckle-sized heads bob in circles with a closed-eye look.

How could my mother do this to us? Chow mein and pigeon soup. I return to the hallway. The pins are set up but no one is playing. At nightfall, by the time the sons and daughter return from hell, the house will be loud with the racket of a family-of-seven's happiness. I will play along. I will look happy, roll my eyes so that only whites show, and roll the ball and count my score on my fingers.

Who's the saint who protects us from the poor?

Dining in Fresno

Yesterday I drove the 180 miles from Berkeley to Fresno, my hometown, to visit my friend Jon Veinberg and talk with him about the super-eight movie we were planning about a 60s rock group to be called The Ministers of Love. In short, we were thinking of a comedy.

When I arrived it was late afternoon. We had a few beers in front of the TV, and toward dusk we left the house to have dinner at a Basque restaurant, Yturri. Since it was a weekday, business was slow. There was a young couple along the wall and two families with elbows on the table, waiting. Flies circled between the dining rooms.

The waitress hurried over, plucked two menus from the side of the cash register, and showed us to a table along the wall. We took a customary peek at the menu, although we both knew we were going to order deep-fried chicken. You couldn't beat the price; it was six-fifty for a five course meal, with coffee and the choice of three kinds of ice cream to wash it all down.

We gave our orders, and soon dipped spoons into lentil soup and rowed for our lives. Scraped two kinds of salad onto our plates, vinegary lettuce and potato. Clunked chunks of stew onto our plates, green beans and garbanzo beans. Tore pieces of French bread we buttered entirely yellow, and talked and ate like Romans. We raised industrial-thick wine glasses to one another, slurped water, and sighed for the good life. When the chicken came, piled a foot high on a plate, I waved mine off and asked the waitress to bring me a doggie bag. She smiled and remarked, "Big boys can't do it?"

"Whoa," said Jon, uncomfortably stuffed. I smiled, patted my belly like a trucker, and pushed my chair back.

We ordered coffee and were talking about friends when the obese family at one end of the long table in the middle of the room began to make faces at a skinny family who, in turn, soured their faced at the fatties. Finally, the oldest son of the fatties got up calmly, walked a few husky steps toward the other family, and ripped the cigarette out of the father's mouth.

"What the hell!" the father said in a restrained voice, getting halfway up, eye ragged with anger.

With a snicker on his face, the fat son returned to take his place with his family. His own father pretended nothing had happened while his mother, square box in a muu-muu, turned to one of her daughters, and muttered, "The guy can't even read. 'No smoking' sign right above his gourd. I swear."

"You better watch it, turkey," the father of the skinnys said, jabbing an angry finger. His face was pink and excited. "You hear me?" He stood glaring while his family—wife, two daughters, and his own son—played with their salad forks, eyes down, embarrassed. Finally the father sat down and picked up his fork.

Jon and I looked at one another, half-snickering.

"Did you see that?" I asked in a low voice. "Slapped that cigarette right out of his mouth."

Jon wagged his head. "I've been telling you for years, Fresno's crazy."

Both families began to mutter and throw ugly glances at each other. Finally the waitress asked the skinnys what the beef was. Pointing fingers sprung up like spears, followed by accusations and more pink faces. The waitress listened like a school teacher and disappeared into the kitchen to return with four liters of house wine—two for each family. She poured gurgling wine into stout wine glasses, which the adults gripped like clubs. Soon they returned to their meals and talk of work and daily matters, though occasionally one would steal a glance at the other family.

We finished our coffee, rolled ice from our water glasses in our mouths as we hoped something would happen, so we could step in and tell them to act like people, not wild animals. But nothing happened. Jon stubbed out his cigarette; I finished my wine. We left with our doggie bags, and instead of heading home right away we started to walk around the block to work off dinner.

It was a pleasant summer evening. The moon was a broken tooth hanging over the Fresno Ice Company; the wind was cool against our faces. What a life, I thought. We sauntered like tourists as we pointed out run-down houses, vacant lots, warehouses we'd love to give our names to. We were talking about a boarded-up machine shop when a squeaking Pinto full of black guys slowed to a stop in the middle of the street. We also slowed to a stop. They looked at us, the red coals of their cigarettes coming and going, and didn't say anything. I knew what this meant; if we continued walking they'd jump us for the three or four dollars in Jon's wallet, and the twenties in mine. Without looking at one another, Jon and I turned around, took a few nonchalant steps, but hurried away when they called us to help push-start their car, an old trick I myself had used in high school. We ran back to the neon glare of the restaurant—ran because we loved our faces as they were, not bloodied or pounded like first-grade clay.

We stood at the entrance, hands on hips, and waited to catch our breath. Jon said, "You're lucky that you live in Berkeley. There ain't a damn thing to do in this town, except get beat up." This was true. In Berkeley you could go to the symphony, maybe a poetry reading, or a foreign movie. You could take in the evening and return home alive. In Fresno, once rated the worst city in the United States by the Rand-McNally Report, you could go out for dinner and later be thrown from a speeding car, quite dead.

We went back inside hoping the skinnys and fatties were so drowned in house wine that when they saw us, blurry friends of the same dinner, they would motion us over to choose sides and fight for the simple thrill of being alive.

Shopping in the 80s

It appears that more and more supermarkets are ushering in Singles Night shopping. I haven't gone to one, mainly because I'm married, but also because there's not a market near me that has come up with such a gimmick. I would certainly like to wheel a cart around and see what the hubbub is all about. A friend, though, has gone, and although he took advantage of the coupons cut from newspaper and magazines, he ran into a problem. While he was looking for a woman, he could only attract come-ons from other men, some of whom looked like women and were in fact more beautiful than women, but underneath it all, well, it just wasn't the same.

Single nights. You kill two birds with one stone. You can do your weekly shopping and flirt, make a date, or if it's love at first sight, hold hands near the racks of tortillas. If you're really romantic you can pet heavily between the rows of international food and even knock jars of escargot, liver pate, and grape leaves off the shelves. The manager with his feather-duster will think nothing of it. The stock boy will continue stomping on cardboard. They've seen it all and, anyway, they quit in ten minutes.

I'd be willing to go. But whereas my friend's intention was to pick up on the opposite sex, my intentions would be strictly sociological. I want to find out what women eat, which would possible lead me to what women want. I would take a cart, search the horizon of flags and sale items—the cokes, the Andre pink Champagne, the Nabisco crackers—for a woman to follow. Let her be a blonde, though a redhead or a brunette would be suitable. Actually, I wouldn't care what she looked like, since my intentions are scientific. Beauty is not the issue.

Let's suppose that the woman I follow, the blonde, picks up a can of soup and it's a generic brand, 12 cents cheaper, and packaged in a white label, so that everyone knows she's a miser. On closer inspection I notice that it's cream of mushroom, which I loathe. Would this mean I would loathe her too; that on a Saturday afternoon, after a football game with the guys, I would come home, shower, and sit at the table to a bowl of cream of mushroom soup, say very quietly that while I sort of like the cheese sandwich, which has its own faults like being too cold and too boring—I simply loathe the soup and, baby, I'm having second thoughts about you.

But I can't think such thoughts. I once went out with a girl who liked cream of mushroom soup, and she was all right, good looking in fact, and bright in a way that mushroom soup is stupid.

Back to sociology. Say I follow the blonde, and she's now fooling with bundles of spinach, which I could live with if cooked right, and is squeezing avocados, which I love, especially mashed in a tortilla, with a sprinkle of cheese and salsa. I go up to her and say, "Hi," and she offers a "Hi," which may or may not mean that she likes me, but is certainly enough of an introduction to allow me to say, "I like avocados too, especially in a tortilla, with a sprinkle of cheese, and salsa." I wait for her to respond. She says "Hi" again, which allows me to say something more clever. I can't think of anything. I stare at her hair, then her forehead. She looks at my cart and asks, "How come it's empty?"

So what if it doesn't work out with the blonde, and so what if my cart is empty? I can fill it up, throw in some expensive meats, three or four watermelons, cake mix, a ten-volume encyclopedia that's on sale, some more meat—and all the while I cruise the aisle, my head bobbing to the rhythm of a brunette's pear-shaped bottom. She looks over her shoulder, and smiles, which is enough for me to say that I like pears but loathe cream of mushroom soup, and hey, look at me, I'm buying these encyclopedias.

I bump into her cart, and she giggles at this. "I hope you have insurance," she charms, and I charm back, "I hope you have insurance too," which is lame but all I can think of to say. I look at her load of groceries, and it's not groceries but mostly paper towels and aluminum foil, and, yes, fourteen tubes of glue. I begin to wonder. She sees what I see, and says that she's a third grade teacher and it's crafts week. "Oh," I say, and stop my cart as I recall the elementary school teacher I once dated. She was no fun at all. She kept telling me to sit up and to stop chewing my fingernails. I tell myself that I probably won't like this woman. I don't know how to get rid of her except to stare, empty-headed, at the Folger's coffee—stare and stare, even when she asks if I'm OK. Finally she gets the message that I don't want her around and rolls her cart away.

I start my cart again, picking up things as I go, peanut butter and olive oil, another melon, and nearly run my cart into a display of potato chips when an attractive woman in short hair and a delicious overbite turns into my aisle and stops before the pickles. I hurry over, pick up the jar of Sweet Butter Chip pickles, the same brand she has, and remark, "Well, what do you know, you like them too?" I then add, "Hi." She says "Hi," which leads me to say, "You drink milk too? What a coincidence!" She has two half-gallon, non-fat milks. She also has a carton of butter, yogurt and canned beans.

While we roll our carts up and down the aisles, I do most of the talking, in fact I do all the talking, which leads me to believe that she's shy and very modest, and that maybe she was hurt by an old boyfriend, some cruel guy who liked doing wheelies on his motorcycle with her on the back.

"Do you live around here?" I ask.

She rolls her cart.

"I like movies that are made into books, don't you?"

She rolls her cart.

"I once had a dog named Brownie, and the funny thing is that he was mostly white."

She rolls her cart and turns into an aisle warm with bread smells. The girl with paper towels and aluminum foil is there. "Hi," I say to her, and she turns rudely away and picks up a loaf of sourdough French bread, which for a moment I think she's going to hit me with. "What's with her?" I tell the attractive woman who, I discover, has left my side and is now in the produce section, weighing tomatoes. I roll my cart over. I pick up a tomato and sniff it for its freshness. "That's funny, I don't smell anything," I wrinkle up my face and tell my new friend, who more and more I'm thinking of as my girlfriend, that the produce here is lousy, and it's better that we just dine out.

For the first time I notice that she's not moving. She's staring at the tomatos. I wave a hand before her eyes. "Are you OK?" Her breathing has stopped. She stares and stares until I roll away, hurt because I realize that she's given me the brush-off. I'm so hurt that I pull my cart into Aisle 8, Cereals, and leave it there, and head to the express line with a six-pack of Bud. The clerk, in the kind of wig Little Richard wears, asks me why I'm so sad. The change falls from the coin dispenser. "I just broke up with my girlfriend," I tell her.

"Ah, that's a shame," she says, "young guy like you."

"Yeah, it's a cryin' shame, but what can you do?"

Agreeable

A friend says that half the world is crazy and the other half are women. That makes sense. Another friend says our problem is that we men never gave a hoot when our mothers tried to teach us how to tie our shoes. Now look at us; we can't go a block without bending over to retie. That makes sense, too. At Thanksgiving my stepfather, drunk and slouched in his chair, says that the Russians made the air bad and the Chinese, if they wanted, could all jump up and down and throw the earth into a panicky spin. I raise my beer and agree.

I'm in my 30s. I'm arguing less and less. Let people be right, even if they're dead wrong. When another friend said that while literature has its 10 gifts for the people, music is the superior art form, I raised my wine glass, and said, "yes, that sounds about right." I took a sip, placed my glass on a book-strewn coffee table, and asked him how he knew. He twirled his empty wine glass and said, I just have a feeling. I told him that that was how I worked. I have hunches and I go by them, like the time I decided to marry a beautiful woman who would feed me balanced meals and love me more than anyone else in the world because I loved her more than anyone else. My friend told me I was lucky, and I agreed that I was lucky but that he was even luckier because his feelings seemed more acute than mine. I filled his wine glass, with a pinkish zinfandel, and he said, thank you.

Only last week there was a tenure meeting. The professors marched in one by one, sat down, looked around, rattled papers, blew their noses, and raised their heads when the chairwoman called the meeting to order. Reviews were read on research and teaching. Everyone slumped down like the dead; three fell asleep, one picked lint from his sweater. The reviews came to an end and the real discussion began. The wave of sentiment rose one way, then another, then flattened to foam, and I was just a bubble in that wave, which snapped when a bearded colleague cried, "No, he's not *realized.*" I agree, I said to myself, he's not realized; let's get rid of him. Then a bald colleague with a twitch in his left eye rose and roused another wave, saying that the colleague up for tenure was in fact more realized than anyone else in his field. I joined the other bubbles to become a large, salty, unstoppable wave. Yeah, I agreed, he's in fact absolutely realized, let's keep him. In the end, he was voted for tenure, and when I saw him the next day in the hallway I clapped him on the shoulder and said, "way to go."

I'm in agreement. We're *all* right. My neighbor who lets his cat feast on my garbage is right. The service mechanic who says my car needs new tires is right. The kids who kicked the smile from my pumpkin are right.

For years I've wanted a pit bull very badly, so badly that I've offered to buy my wife furs, a car, expensive shoes, a new kitchen if she'd agree to our getting one. But she always argued that I was weird to want a pit bull. I threatened divorce, she vacuumed the floor. I threatened to have our daughter baptized Catholic, she did the dishes. I sulked like a toad and then whined that all the black guys at the karate studio had pit bulls and why couldn't I. I slammed the door, raced my car around the block, and came home in time for dinner.

But I agree with her. I don't need a pit bull. I could use

one, but it's not that important. I could use a punching bag in the back yard, and a new bike. I would love to go to France this fall, but I must be reasonable. I'm 34 and it's time for me to act my age.

I've been practicing, too. The other day my wife and I went to a poetry reading and sat through an hour of a very loud poet counting off on her fingers her rotten, no-good lovers. She needed six hands. I grew bored. I went into myself and started to wonder why she kept picking the same kind of men, most of them married with alcoholic hairlines. But I stopped my thoughts, shooed them away like flies. I wanted to agree with her. I applauded when it was over and was nice enough to buy her book.

I'm no longer a loud mouth, a sucker-puncher, the first one at the party and the last one to go home. I've become agreeable. Even my wife seems happy with me. She's setting rows of pepperoni on a pizza. She smiles, and I hug her. We agree that we love one another. She asks, "Do you want to go to a movie?" "Yes," I say. "What do you want to see?" "Anything," I say, squeezing her waist. How about something scary, she asks. My hands scuffle up to her breasts. Yes, honey, yes to everything.

Pets

Our first pet was Boots, an orange cat with a triangle-shaped head and teeth like a snake's, and who in fact became the snake of evilness when he ate Pete, our 25 cent canary from Woolworths, a painted bird that dripped his artificial colors when he played in a tuna can of water. Pete faded right before our eyes, and seemed to chirp less and less, as if he himself had discovered that he was not exotic but just a plain yellow canary and no kin to the toucan or jungle-tree hummingbird. We liked him, nevertheless, especially when he gargled his seeds and jumped around in circles.

One evening Mom and we kids returned home to find the cage turned on its side, one bird's leg, twig-thin, on the floor, feathers floating in the air, and Boots on the dining table, blinking a set of satisfied eyes. The clues were in. Mom's eyes widened with anger as she swung at Boots. Poor cat, he went flying and, instead of on his feet, he landed on his head, scrambled, shrieked, and ran, literally, up the wall, almost touching the ceiling.

I liked Boots. She let us put flowers behind her ears and a paper cape on her back, and let us wrap her paws in aluminum foil so that she rustled when she walked. Space cat, we thought, she looks like she's from space. We were happy with ourselves, and crazy with laughter when we wrapped her entire body in aluminum. When she walked, she showered pieces of light and made a clinking sound like dragged chains. We were very sad when she ran away one day.

I liked Boots but liked our dog Blackie better, even though he would never allow us to wrap him in aluminum and play our space game. He had no special talent, except he was warm to hold. Being old, he slept mostly, drank water, moaned instead of barked, and wobbled when he trotted after us up the alley, thinking that perhaps we were leading him to food. He was the only dog we knew who liked raisins. That was his breakfast, and our breakfast too, with cereal or a buttered tortilla for us, and scraps for him. Raisins. They were free since our parents worked at Sun-Maid Raisins and they could bring boxes home as they pleased. Blackie also liked oranges and sometimes even dried apricots. Years later, when we got another dog and fed him fruit that he only looked at, I assumed he was ill and that he would go away like Pete and Boots and Blackie himself.

Blackie was hit by a car. My uncle was the first to find him and probe his belly and its bulb of blood. My brother and sister were there, with free pickles fished out of open barrels from the Coleman Pickle Company. It was summer, dusk, the west a pinkish streak where the sun went down. I didn't know about Blackie until Uncle had him in his arms and was carrying him down the alley where I waited for our Japanese neighbor to go inside so I could steal plums. But I forgot about the plums and joined the procession, petting Blackie's head and asking him if he was OK—did it hurt, did he want some raisins—and asking my uncle what he was going to do with Blackie. Uncle didn't say anything. We walked past the broom factory and its *wham wham* of machinery that tied straw to bright colorful sticks that became brooms.

We kids stopped at Van Ness and were told to stay there, to go home if we wanted, or wait, but not to dare cross the street because we might become like Blackie. Rick and Debra left in time, but I stayed and counted the *wham whams*, and

112

thought that every four made one broom. That's a lot of brooms, I thought, more brooms than people. But soon I lost count and thought only of Blackie and where he was going. I was sad and scared, and wanted to cross the street but knew better. Uncle came back without our dog but with peaches. When I asked him where Blackie went, he said that he was living at another house with a happy family. Where, I asked, and he pointed, over there, and *there* was nothing but a dark outline of warehouses and poor houses, now that there was very little light.

I was four when we got him and six when we let him go. Father let me name him. I didn't know my colors very well at the time and chose Blackie, even though he was mostly brown like me and my brother and sister and the raisins that were in no way an afternoon snack but real food for the living.

Summer Night

I'm returning home from a softball game, late. I'm thirteen and the mitt on my handlebars is older than I. My bike is older, and our car, a Woody station wagon, is older. My sister, a year younger than I, *looks* older in her first bra and fixed up in make-up that's more like cuts and bruises than beauty. She even eats sunflower seeds like the older kids, slowly, one at a time, spitting the shells like boyfriends who don't work out.

I lean my bike against the garage and hurry to the bathroom because Andy, a kid from the other street, is hiking a new girl on his handlebars, and now they're making out with their eyes closed. I turn on the bath water, undress while eating a plum, and step into the bathtub. I look around; there's nothing to do.

God's away right now but he's coming back soon, a voice whispers to me inside my head, as I get comfortable in the tub, steam rising off the milky surface. My penis is engorged, and I'm thinking should I or shouldn't I? No. It's all right, another voice tells me in my left ear. Go ahead and do it. I do it without looking, though I can hear the small waves of the water licking the edges of the bathtub. When I look down at the renegade sperm on the water, a voice says, God saw you. Shame spots my face. I feel very bad and feel even worse when my penis cools off, collapsing like a very skinny tent. Depressed, I drain the water, towel off, and notice my spindly tufts of hair, which were not there six months ago—notice that they're like beards of steel wool, the kind I use to shine my bike, which will always be older than I am. I'm even more depressed.

I go outside to the front yard. It's late, still hot and, except for the crickets in the holly bush, quiet. I start up the street. Where is everyone? Before my bath there were kids and parents and lawn-sniffing dogs. My own mother was watering on the side of the house, and now she's gone. I even remember Rick sitting on top of our Woody, trying to look cool in a pair of sun glasses he found at the playground. For a second I think I'm in hell for doing it; that God said, watch this, Gary—and made all the good people disappear.

There's only a Mr. Grycz, who's shirtless on his front steps. Sweat is running like wild ants down his meaty shoulders. When he coughs, something like a wheelbarrow of rocks rattles in his chest. His wife Jutte, with a forearm strong enough to grate blocks of industrial-size cheese, is reading a gray newspaper by an orange porchlight. She looks up at me as I pass. She flicks a finger of sweat at the ground. Her teeth are orange, and scary, like wax vampire teeth seen for the first time. My mother, a dragon with her curses, likes to scare us by saying that if we don't get Bs on our report cards, we're going to be like them—miserable.

"Where did everybody go?" I ask. Jutte shrugs her shoulders and says, "They go to hell"—the husband and wife laugh, and I laugh too because they're spooky. I think I should get on the good side of them. Laugh, take a step back. Laugh, laugh, take a step—until I'm out of sight but thinking that their marriage is older than my bike or the trees or the devil himself, who likes to hang around the bathtub and say things like, go ahead, God's not looking.

I want to have a girl right now. Andy once told me it was like greasy chicken, and after he told me I went around not liking girls very much. It seemed awful. In bed I kept picturing a hot, bald, salt-and-peppered chicken attached to my penis, and my brother in the bunk above me asking, "What's going on?"—and me telling him I just can't get comfortable because it's hot. Of course, God would be looking, no two ways about it, and He would whisper, maybe call out loud enough for Mom to hear, "Leave the chicken alone, Gary."

But, then again, Andy would know because he's had his time with the daughter of the peanut man, the one who works the mall. He's poor as they come: one leg shorter than the other, and pitiful trying to sell peanuts in a town that's in love with sunflower seeds.

I remember when Andy had started liking her. He had asked me to help him carry cardboard boxes from Pete's Grocery and, bored with killing ants with a concoction of gasoline and pink stuff in a bottle I found in the garage, I said, "Okie-Doke." We hauled the boxes over our heads to the yard of an abandoned house on Orchard Street. He set the cardboard in weeds and stomped them into a bed, and placed a brick at each corner so that they wouldn't fly away. He also dug a hole where he was going to hide some cokes, along with a bag of sunflowers seeds, even though he didn't think he'd have to eat the seeds because his girl was bringing peanuts.

But where is Andy and that new girl now? Did he crash his bike and die with her in his arms? Where are my brother and sister? Mom was just now watering the yard, and now she's gone. It's eerie when there are no other kids around to beat you up.

Then they all arrive, in the back of Mr. Wise's pickup, though Mother's in the cab. They've been to a fire. Everyone is happy and excited, as if they've been holding their breath. Cross-eyed Johnny is the first to leap from the truck, as it squeaks into the drive, and the first to tell me that a house on Belmont Avenue burned to the floor and though no one died,

116

at least three people cried, and ain't that better than nothing?
God's going to get his way, in time, in time.

A Short History of Sex

"Hijo, this is the light switch. No pay you bill, no light, and you make babies with no light." This was Grandmother telling me about sex, or hinting about how sex works. If you don't pay up to the PG&E, then all there is to do at night is lie in bed and make love. This was my first introduction to cause and effect, how one thing leads to another. I was eleven, eating a peach from her tree and watching her water the lawn that was so green it was turning blue. Grandma turned the hose on me, said "Now you be a good boy and play." She squirted me as I ran around the yard with my jaw gripping the peach and my hands covering my eyes.

It was different with my mother, who broke the news about sex while folding clothes in the garage. "You get a girl pregnant, and I'll kill you." No logic there, just a plain simple Soto threat. I felt embarrassed because we had never talked about sex in the family. I didn't know what to do except to stare at the wall and an old calendar of an Aztec warrior eye-balling his girlfriend's breasts. I left the garage, got on my bike and did wheelies up and down the street, trying my best to get run over because earlier in the week Sue Zimm and I had done things in Mrs. Hancock's shed. It was better, I thought, that I should die on my own than by my mother's hand.

But nothing happened. Sue only got fat from eating and I

got skinny from worrying about the Russians invading the United States. I thought very little about girls. I played base-ball, looked for work with a rake and poor-boy's grin, and read books about Roman and Greek gods.

During the summer when I was thirteen I joined the YMCA, which was a mistake—grown men swam nude there and stood around with their hands on their hips. It was an abominable exhibition, and I would have asked for my money back but was too shy to approach the person at the desk. Instead, I gave up swimming and jumped on the trampoline, played basketball by myself, and joined the Y "combatives" team, which was really six or seven guys who got together at noon to beat up one another. I was gypped there too. I could have got beaten up for free on my street; instead, I rode my bike three miles to let people I didn't even know do it to me.

But sex kept coming back in little hints. I saw my mother's bra on the bedpost. I heard watery sounds come from the bathroom, and it wasn't water draining from the tub. At lunch time at school I heard someone say, "It feels like the inside of your mouth." What feels like that? I wanted to ask, but instead ate my sandwich, drank my milk, kicked the soccer ball against the backstop, then went to history, where I studied maps, noting that Russia was really closer than anyone ever suspected. It was there, just next to Alaska, and if we weren't careful they could cross over to America. It would be easy for them to disguise themselves as Eskimos and no one would know the difference, right?

In high school I didn't date. I wrestled for school, the Roosevelt Rough Riders, which was just young guys humping one another on mats. I read books, ate the same lunch day after day, and watched for Mrs. Tuttle's inner thighs above her miniskirt, thinking, "It's like the inside of your mouth." I watched her mouth; her back teeth were blue with shadows, and her tongue was like any other tongue, sort of pink. By then I wanted a girl very badly. Once almost had a girlfriend except she moved away, leaving me to mope around the school campus eating spam sandwiches with the ugly boys.

My mother's bra on the bedpost, my sister now with breasts that I could almost see beneath her flannel nightgown. One night my brother bragged that he knew for sure it felt like a mouth and in fact was drippy like a marble coated with motor oil. In the dark I scrunched up my face as I remembered cross-eyed Johnny's sock of sweaty marbles, for which I had traded three bottles of red stuff from a chemistry kit.

I had to have a girl. I was desperate. I stuffed kleenex in my pants pocket and went around with no shirt. I thought of Sue Zimm. But she was now lifting weights and looking more like a guy than a girl, which confused me. I was even more confused when George from George's Barber rubbed my neck and asked me how it felt. I told him it felt OK. He asked if I was going steady, and I told him that I sort of was, except my girl had moved away. He said that it was better that way because sometimes they carried disease you couldn't see for a long time until it was too late. This scared me. I recalled touching Sue when I was thirteen, and wasn't it true that she coughed a lot? Maybe something rubbed onto me. Biting a fingernail I walked home very slowly, with a picture of a scolding priest playing inside my head. At home I noticed mom coughing as she stirred a pot of beans. Fear ran its icy fingers up and down my back. I gave my mom the disease, I said to myself, and went to hide in my room and talk to God about becoming a priest.

Years passed without my ever touching a girl. My brother seemed to get them all, especially when we roomed together in college and he would bring them home. I was studying history, then, things like, "In 1940 Britain invaded Tibet; in 1911 the first Chinese revolution began; about that time, people began to live longer because they had learned to wash their hands before eating." I would hover over a big book with few pictures while my brother and his girl went at it, howling so loudly that our cat would stir from sleep and saunter to the bedroom door and holler some meows herself.

I was twenty, the only guy left who went around eating spam sandwiches in college, when I had my first girlfriend who didn't move away. I was a virgin with the girl whom I would marry. In bed I entered her with a sigh, rejoiced "Holy, holy" to my guardian angel, and entered her again with the picture of a tsk-tsking priest playing inside my head.

Twenty years, I thought. It's nothing like cross-eyed Johnny's sock of sweaty marbles. And I couldn't believe what it looked like. While my girl slept, I lowered myself onto an elbow and studied this peach mouth, squeeze thing, little hill with no Christian flag. Pussy was what they called it: a cat that meowed and carried on when you played with it very lightly.

A Local Issue

I remember Grady, my first black friend, running naked from Mrs. Hill, the eighth-grade teacher, his teacher in other words—running because she had a question to ask him and, I guess, the question couldn't wait for him to get dressed. It was Friday, after our last P.E. class, and Grady and I and some other kids were playing two on two basketball with a volley ball. We won by twelve points, even when we spotted the other kids points and made a rule that we could only walk not run. We went in to shower. Naked and turning circles in a blue-cold shower, squealing that the water was freezing, Mrs. Hill's face loomed large in the shower room. Her shoes were getting wet from the spray. Her glasses were misted over.

"Grady," she said, "your mother and I are going to meet on Thursday. . ."

An embarrassed Grady screamed and ran past her and took a left into the locker room. With another kid I hurried to the corner of the shower and tried to hide in the musty shadows. I crouched down, the guy next to me cussing up a storm, and looked down at my thing, small band-aid of flesh. I was already having problems adjusting to the tufts of hair that were down there, tufts that threw out a few thin shadows so that it seemed I had more, but in fact for a seventh grader I was bald as a plucked chicken.

Didn't she know better not to come into the gym? Perhaps not. She was old, senile perhaps, the kind of teacher who spits at you when she talks and eats sandwiches while her class reads a poem from a book no one understands even though the words are easy. Old and senile and the object of ridicule at the school assembly on the last day of school. When the principal announced that she would be retiring, the bad boys—the cholos first, then the surfer boys who were really Okies—began to clap, hoot and holler. The French Club and the school band joined in, and the Chicanas with the black flags of mascara over their eyes snapped their gum and nodded their heads. They were too cool to be loud.

Grady and our eighth grade summer. Trouble started when we sailed inner tubes down the Mayfair canal and ended up in Clovis, a white cowboy town where it was not uncommon to see people on horseback. The people blinked at us, and we blinked back and offered feeble waves that did us no good. In short, we didn't belong, brown boy and black kid on the wrong side of town. The cops had to drive us back to Fresno; we worried all the way home with our heads down, because we had to leave our inner tubes and they weren't ours but my stepfather's. We'd have to kill ourselves, we thought, maybe play stupid if we were lucky and just shrug our shoulders and drool, when he found them missing from the garage.

But I remember Grady best when his house burned down—just the kitchen and back porch—and a local club held a benefit for his family at Romain Playground, which was only five houses away from us. The club members rolled trailers into the playground, set up lawn chairs and barbecues, and stood around in sun glasses talking small talk.

Two white softball teams, one black family in need. For every hit, Grady's family would get twenty dollars to help reconstruct their house.

A man with a cowboy tie came to the speaker. "Testing. Hello, hello . . . We're all here to play a good game of ball and help our local Negroes." There was clapping, then the

Star Spangled Banner sung by Ann of Ann's Hardware, before the game began with a pop up that ricocheted into the bleachers. On the next pitch it was lifted into left and snapped up very nicely with one hand.

I sat with Grady and his Mom and some kids who looked like Grady, except they were nappy heads and since it was summer wore no shoes. I watched the game for a while, but grew bored, hot, hotly bored and left. I went over to David King's house who was doing a magic trick by making a kleenex dance like tiny night gowns in his living room. I didn't let on, of course, that I could see wire. I tried to look amazed and ask him questions about ghosts and things.

Did Grady's family make much money from the game? I'm not sure. I do remember, though, riding my bike past his house and seeing a pile of new lumber sitting on his lawn. It stayed there for a long time, months maybe, before it disappeared stick by stick. I guess the kitchen was built because from our own kitchen I often saw Grady come out of his house with his mouth chewing the last bites of a hot meal.

How I Cured Myself

A friend writes again:

Only last month I took my wife's suggestion to start analysis, not because I was burned out from my job or even slightly disturbed by a childhood incident that I'd yet to work out. My problem was that I didn't sleep well. Over the years I had tried to cure my insomnia with home remedies: I first sank into the mattress and thought of myself as a body of water. I read difficult books: Plato, Plato's friends, religious treatise, St. Augustine, and medical journals, among many others. I also read easy books: some things by John Updike, Alice Adams, Raymond Carver, and all the mysteries *The New Yorker* said were good. I also read easy but depressing books that so disturbed me that I lay in bed counting the sweeps of headlights on the ceiling, which in my hands-behind-my-head worry I noticed was cracked. This led me to believe that the house's foundation, too, was cracked and was sinking in shallow waters. It would cost me money to hire someone to do the repairs.

I cut back on coffee, the wine with dinner. I stayed away from people who were unusually rude because they bothered me later when I got in bed thinking just how rude they were. I practiced yoga for a week until I hurt my knee. And still, on a bad knee, I took up jogging, which bored me, and lifted plastic weights and hung upside down in gravity boots, which were reportedly not only good for lengthening the spine, draining the lymph glands, and refreshing the blood, but also stretching the muscles so that when you came down you were more relaxed. However, my head spun dizzily, my ears rang, especially the left one, and my tongue seemed more yellow, like a flattened canary, which disturbed me so much that I lost even more sleep.

I took up model ship building as a hobby, bowled with a neighbor, drank Chinese herbal teas, and did sit-ups and push-ups by the hundreds. I joined a reading group which did in fact make my eyes water for sleep and forced me to yawn hat-size yawns. I only woke up when it was time for cookies and punch. At night, nevertheless, it was the same story: my wife snoring up a storm and I awake counting the sweeps of headlights on the cracked ceiling.

I compared childhood sleep, which was wonderful, to adult sleep which was a pair of raw liquid eyes following me around no matter how I hid under the blankets. I would have been happy to settle for something in between.

I turned to the telephone book to search for a psychologist. My hair stood on end. The list was endless, the world being sicker than I imagined. There were marriage counselors, counselors for black-and-white relationships, therapists for business men and women, stress managers, sexologists, bilingual therapists, hypnotists for bulimics, assertiveness training specialists. It disturbed me to know that there were Ph.D.s for teeth grinding and spastic colons.

I let the telephone book fall from my lap. I felt a heavy rock shift inside. I got into my gravity boots and started humming, which a friend said was good for self-awareness. I did feel better, and a lot better when I came down and my dizziness stopped. I drank two glasses of water, did some push-ups, and sat on the couch thumbing through *The New Yorker* in search of the cartoons. I hugged my wife when she came home, helped her with the salad (though I was uneasy cutting the tomatoes, which reminded me of the eyes that lurk under my blankets). But soon the task of tossing the salad cheered me up further. Being happy, I ate like a Roman, tearing at the meat with my teeth, and drank two glasses of wine, which was a mistake because I couldn't sleep that night. In bed I looked over at my wife. I could see that her mouth was open and a noise like a leaf rattling on a windshield was coming from her mouth. I rolled over and looked at the ceiling. It seemed more cracked than ever. I cried to myself as I waited for those eyes to show up again and pester me until dawn.

The next day I searched the bulletin boards at the Co-Op Market for a therapy group, and was lucky enough to find one that seemed for me. I wrote down the number, and went home to hang upside down in my gravity boots and hum. I again felt better, jolly, and played with the dog until my wife drove home. We had an early dinner because she was performing at the Unitarian Church (she plays her violin) that night with the city orchestra, a modest group of really very talented musicians. The violins playing Strauss whined through me, and I thought about how radiation can enter the body, cause cancer, make you lie down even when you want to get up. I crossed my legs and worried about the world.

During the intermission I walked around with an empty paper cup, because I was afraid that if I drank anything I would have problems sleeping. I didn't even drink water, though I pretended to sip so that none of my wife's friends would ask, "Would you like something to drink?" I didn't try the cookies or the salty things. I walked around trying to keep to myself, and glanced at the very orderly bulletin board. I looked for therapy groups. I didn't find any, but did stop in front of a scraggly little note that said "I Listen." That was it. It gave a number and a name, which I thought said Rob but could have been Ron. I listen, I said to myself, I listen. That's certainly different. I sipped from my empty cup as I returned to my seat for the second half of the performance.

That night I glanced at the ceiling but it didn't bother me. I fell asleep, and remained asleep until my wife rolled over and touched my shoulder. I woke groggily but so relieved that I had lain seven hours with my eyes closed. I dressed, went to work, and returned home early to slip into my gravity boots and hum, then play with the dog until my wife returned home. We ate early (no wine). After I did the dishes, I asked my wife to play the violin, which was not the same as hearing an orchestra but helped me sleep that night. And I slept the following night.

I had cured myself. The formula was simple: clamp yourself with gravity boots and hum, play with the dog until the wife comes home, eat dinner, do the dishes, listen to the wife play the violin, and sleep. It was all perfect, like music itself. Habit, I thought. Habit is how things get done. I tapped my foot, clapped to her playing, and tossed my head from side to side. I had cured myself and am almost happy. Now on to other problems.

Lunch in the Business Park

At noon the park benches are a sort of anthology of every form of trouble and well-being: the old man the color of old money, a bored secretary with the title Office Manager II, the giddy just-married woman, the not so giddy much-divorced men eating their three saran-wapped cookies, the black-suited lawyers in pairs, a dusty brick mason, the street person hunkering into his drab coat, the Tai Chi master resting with a towel around his neck—most of them weighing down the benches with the smell of life's slapped-together lunches. There's the woman reading a how-to cook book, another a romance novel, and there's the man whose pant legs ride up his ankles reading the back of a milk carton. It must be engaging to know that the milk was processed in Stockton, because he can't take his eyes off the carton.

I don't mean to gossip, but I think that man over there, the one with his coat off, who's thirtyish, neither good-looking nor bad-looking, has just broken up with his girlfriend. He has the look of a deflated inner-tube hanging on a nail in a garage. He chews his sandwich slowly, absent-mindedly, and doesn't look up. He sips on his straw; he pulls back the slice of bread, as one might the lips of a horse to inspect the teeth. Let me speculate on his sorrow. He was bored, dead bored, and was foolish enough to tell his girlfriend, a rabbit-faced blond who works as a buyer for a paper company. She wasn't so bored to let him get away with that and tossed him out. Now he's not so bored, but he feels worse. And let's not speak of the mustard on his left cheek.

That woman in the pleated black dress doesn't look so snappy, either. She spoons her yoghurt like a baby, one slow bite at a time. Maybe she has a hangover. I notice that when I suffer from staying out late, I eat slowly too. Sludge slides from my brain; my arms feel weak and my tongue is a dead furry mouse. But my guess is that she's lonely which is worse than being bored, but not so bad as having no place to live, like that guy stretched out on the lawn. This woman has been married once, almost twice, and dates infrequently. Last Friday she balanced her checkbook and managed to do her laundry in one load. Last Thursday she watched television until 11:00. Last Wednesday she washed her panties in the bathroom sink and let them drip their gray, weeping tears from a hanger in the shower.

I don't want to depress myself. Let me tell you about the happiest person in this park. Actually it's no person at all, but a dog who's nibbling a hamburger with fries on the side. I don't know how the mutt got his lunch, but when I arrived at the park he was going to town on the burger—the cheese like tangled yarn between his yapping jaws. When he takes a fry in his mouth, it's like a cigarette. Gangster dog, happy dog. When I call, "Hey, Charlie," he looks up, wags his tail, looks back down to where his hamburger is. When I call, "Hey Freckles," he looks up, wags his tail, scratches, and looks back down. He responds to any name because it might mean food. He's eating for the love of eating, and the love of his flesh, which is glossy without a hair out of place. What other man or woman in this park could say the same?

I'm not as happy as this dog, but I've gone to 12:05 mass, have given a bag lunch away to a poor man, and have flirted with a saleswoman in a toystore. I was out getting typing paper. I saw her from the street straightening up stuffed bears, went in, and asked about the electric robots with rotating eyes, then a baby that spoke back and had the power to wet its diapers. We stood by the stuffed animals and talked. Yes, I like Chinese food. Yes, I like dancing. Yes, I have a car and sometimes suffer from insomnia. In the end, I bought the How-and-Why Wonder Book of Dinosaurs, but not before I asked for her phone number. I don't know what to do with it. I'm married, after all, father to a smart child, and Catholic. The scales of sin are heaped with sharp rocks. It's delicious trouble that I want, and a park bench. I am happy, bark out my happiness, and ruffle up the dog's fur as I leave to return home.

Literary Criticism

The book was long, extremely long, and took me three nights to read. One of those nights I spent with Sarah, who kept poking my arm and asking, "What are you reading?" An extremely long book, I said, and tenderly pinched her nose, which is dented like a boxer's but cute, and told her to go to sleep, that I had some reading to do. Instead of rolling over, she picked up her *Vogue* and started thumbing pages, which distracted me. I kept glancing over to each new page of glossy lingerie ads. I loved the one with a woman, in a pointy bra and flower-pink panties, standing on a stagecoach, with her hand shading her brow and looking west. Well, I live in the West, I thought. She's looking for me. I chuckled to myself and put my novel down; I scooted close to Sarah, who looked up and smiled.

"That's a funny ad, huh?" I said. She smiled wide; the dents in her face filled with dark shadows. We looked at the magazine together, got horny, and then went at one another with great gusto. After it was over, Sarah did fall asleep and I went back to my book, which if you should know is about a man and a woman living extremely long lives. On page three, they are playmates at school; on page fourteen they are in junior high and sitting across from one another in the school orchestra, he with a trombone, she with the flute. On page eighty they are married and weaving in and out of their midlife crises, which of course means they jump from bed to bed and jog through misty parks to hide their guilt. By page ninety they are divorced; he is living in an apartment with a few sticks of furniture with a girlfriend who's an artist; she drinks a lot of coffee and is obsessed with the neighbor's tree where kids are building a tree house. She wishes they would stop; she thinks they are hurting the limbs. Meanwhile the ex-wife has the house and their two sons, and has a lover who is married to a wife who is very ill and may die as soon as the next paragraph. On page a hundred and thirty they are pretty old, sixty maybe, and I begin to think that this four-hundred-page novel is not about this couple who were neighborhood sweethearts, but maybe their kids, in their twenties, taking a lot of drugs and watching TV with the sound turned down. On page a hundred fifty-two Sarah groggily rises on an elbow, smacks her lips, and asks, "What time is it?" I don't have a clock in the room, but nevertheless tell her it's late, one ten in the morning. She rolls onto her back, and more than any other time her face is dented with dark shadows. But her face lightens when she rolls onto her belly and starts to thumb through her *Vogue*, which of course distracts me immensely. I put down the book and look over her shoulder, which has the faint smell of perfume. I ask her the name of her perfume. She smiles, "What perfume?" I tell her, "The perfume you're wearing." She says that she doesn't wear any and says that I'm a silly boy. She kisses me and asks me to go peel her an orange.

The next night I'm alone at the dining table with the novel, which I must read in order to do my review. I read thirty pages and find out the novel is in fact about their children; the parents were just a warm-up for things to come. I make notes; I write a few sentences in my leather-bound pad. I bite my pencil, furrow my brow, and think in symbols. The book is getting pretty good when my cat scratches on the back door and I have to get up and let her in. To my shock my cat is bleeding. I look closer. I go down to a knee, take her head into my hands, and see that an ear is gone. The blood is pasty. Fear takes me by the collar. I pick her up, stroking her, ask, "What happened?" She meows, and rubs a paw across her nose. I take her to the bathroom, wash her wound, and place her on the bed while I nervously look through the yellow pages for a 24-hour veterinarian. I call, scramble into my clothes, and pick up my cat who has bled on my bed. I've never had a virgin, I think to myself, and pick her up, swaddle her in a bath towel, and drive ten miles to save her life.

The next night is quiet. I read in bed and try to get comfortable. I lie on my stomach and my neck hurts. I sit up, with pillows propped up behind, and my neck still hurts. I cross my legs, do a yoga stretch, and start reading about the kids who have turned off the TV and started off on careers. This stops abruptly. My cat leaps into my lap; I toss her away delicately. She leaps back into my lap. I toss her away, this time less delicately. She leaps back on and I toss her away, almost violently. But I catch myself, big meany, and begin to feel for her. I take her into my arms. She has a football helmet of white tape on her head. When she meows, hardly any sound comes out. When she walks, she staggers from left to right. I coo into the ear that's left, "Poor kitty."

Finally, after my cat has fallen asleep, I pick up the novel and read about the children who have gone on to great success, despite the broken home they've come from. Jerry, better known as Biff by his friends, has become a well-liked doctor who works in Emergency. He is married, but would prefer to be gay. His younger brother Jaro is a big-time advertiser in a small town. He likes his clothes, his car, his swimming pool with its non-skid bottom. Now if only he loved his wife, his life would be perfect. But he doesn't like her. She smokes too much, and hacks in her sleep.

I make some notes in my pad. I stroke my cat, drink from the glass of water on the night stand, and return to reading about how their marriages fall apart. What is the author saying? I bite my yellow pencil, and deep-stitch my brow with intelligence. I scratch in my pad, What Is The Author Saying? I underline it, and continue reading about their love affairs, which depress me, because I've always wanted to speed in residential streets and flirt with death on mountainous curves.

The book ends on a high note: Biff comes out of the closet, with a streaming banner of gay pride, and Jaro divorces his wife, sells his advertising agency, and disappears in a large cosmopolitan city where it seems every third person is named Jaro.

I snap closed my book, stretch and yawn noisily, and cuddle my cat who lets out a soundless meow. Boy, that was a good book. I kick back the blankets, slip into my slippers, and, with my cat staggering alongside, go into the kitchen for a glass of milk. I pour kitty a saucer of milk, and together we drink. Leaning against the sink, I think about symbols and how true they are. I'm like my cat, in her football helmet of white tape. My hurt is in the head too, but it can't be seen until I meet a woman and my despair gushes out on the second or third date. I drink my milk; my cat drinks her milk. Symbols, I think, symbols. My cat looks up with beads of milk on her whiskers, and meows. I meow back and wipe my mouth with my sleeve.

Together we go to bed. I reread the chapter about loneliness while she licks her paws and stares at the page, which means nothing to her and almost nothing to me, now that I have to pick up my pen and be like everyone else and say something very, very bad.

A Weekend

I thought sailing was something my family would like to do on weekends. Others have tennis, some bowling, others television, still others bowling and television. But it was the blue that I wanted, sea-salt in our hair, and the jib popping overhead as the boat, a twenty-five foot Mercury yacht, cut right, no starboard I mean, with wind blowing so hard that it's difficult to catch our breath. I wanted the sun, bright coin over the Bay Bridge, and maybe flat layers of Godly fog. Perch could jump like dreams from green water, and California seals stare at us from moss-dark rocks where no boats would dare venture.

One Saturday when the Cal Sailing Club was giving free rides, I suggested that we go. Since my in-laws were visiting, I thought that it would be something pleasant to do. My father-in-law said, "No water for me," as he was scared of boats, even in a dinky bay with five-inch waves, but if Carolyn would go with him he wouldn't mind trying his luck at Golden Gate Fields. My mother-in-law, the most polite person I know, said that she was game; my daughter leaped into my arms, she was so happy to finally go sailing.

While my wife and my father-in-law went their way, we drove to the Berkeley pier, stood in line and kicked gravel as we waited forty minutes for our turn. Left to her devices, my daughter wandered near the snack stand where she discovered an ant hole. She squatted to study its activity and noticed that the same three ants were responsible for hauling rice-size pieces of dark earth from the hole. She called me over to look. She was right. The same ants came and went; the others milled around like nervous shoppers.

Finally we were pointed to a boat where an old salt stood peeling bubble gum from the bottoms of his sneakers with a screw driver. As we approached, he looked up, smiled a handful of brown teeth, and said to get in: first my mother-in-law, then the child, then me, and finally the couple behind us, both with cameras slung over their shoulders and sun glasses in their breast pockets.

The slat benches were wet. My daughter looked at me, with a what-should-I-do look. Reluctantly, as I hate wet clothes, I sat down and patted my lap for Mariko to sit. She wriggled onto my lap and jostled for a better view of the oily dock water. My mother-in-law, ever wise, sat on folded news-paper she had brought with her. She put on her hat and smiled at us.

Meanwhile, Old Salt, with the help of a Cal Student, rigged a mast, played with ropes, pulled up anchor, and shouted for us to watch out for the staysail, that it would swing to left, portside, just as we had made our way out of the harbor. And once out of the harbor the sail did swing port-side, and we ducked our heads and grinned.

The wind caught the sails roughly, sending up water that drenched us. Except for Old Salt, all of us screamed and gripped the benches. I looked at Mariko, then my mother-in-law, then the couple whose sun glasses were ripped from their pockets and lay on the deck, that piece of wood that separated us from the sea and certain death. The sailboat dipped again, and we screamed again, using all our throat muscles. Dip, scream; dip, scream.

Glasses off, I wiped my face, grimaced, and was about to warn Mariko to hold on to my belt when again Old Salt warned us to watch for the staysail that was starting its starboard swing. Mariko cowered, pulled her hat down nearly over her eyes, and held on. The sailboat dipped again, leaned dangerously on its side as it picked up speed in the open water, and for the next thirty minutes scared us out of our wits.

Who was most scared? Mariko, my mother-in-law? The couple who left their sun glasses on the deck, not wanting to risk getting them for fear they would be washed out to sea by an unexpected wave? No, it was an *ant* that sat, legs splayed, in a bubble of water on my shoe; an ant from the hole near the snack stand who had apparently crawled onto my shoe and come out to sea for a weekend ride.

My first impulse was to put him out of misery and smear him into a black jam under my thumb. But in between the splashes of water, I became intrigued by this ant, courageous sliver of life, and rooted for him to hang on, that it was only a matter of time before he once again saw land. And he did hang on; we coasted, mainsail down, to the dock. Mariko, who had her face hidden in her hat for most of the ride, came out like a turtle and asked, "Is it almost over?" I patted her lap and said, "Yes."

But we screamed one last time when the boat nudged the dock, not in the least embarrassed by our cowardice. We were happy to be alive, cold as we were, wet as we were. On shaky legs, we walked up the dock toward land, sat on a railroad tie, backs to the Bay, and warmed ourselves by raising our faces skyward. The ant that was once plastered to my shoe came back to life, and crawled slowly back to the dirt. I was careful not to step on him when I rose to leave.

And Carolyn and my father-in-law? They bet everything on the first two races, and for the rest of the afternoon sat on their hands watching everyone around them make money.

Night Sitting

I recall an evening in late September when there was no noise other than crickets, wind and a dry rattle of leaves on a branch. My wife and I were huddled in our robes in the back yard that we had shoveled and watered into blossom all summer. Petunias brightened the back fence and the lantern-like flowers of the fuchsia showered petals in the slightest wind. We had enjoyed apples and apricots, pears and the neighbor's loquats that we picked when they weren't looking. The lawn, a triangle of green, had been cut a dozen times, maybe more; snails pulled from petals were flicked against the fence where they died a watery death in the sun. Less than two weeks ago it had been the usual cool Berkeley summer: low clouds over the hills in the morning and the sun breaking through in the afternoon.

Now it was the beginning of fall. In the dark of the back yard, our light was Carolyn's cigarette, a cap of red that outlined her face when she inhaled. For a while we talked about the day—bills, letter from her mother, letter from a friend in Europe—but eventually we gave ourselves over to the quiet. The stars were faint silvery points; the jets were steely lights cutting east and west. I thought about a friend, five states away, who was really much closer because I could imagine his belly laugh and the raise-and-chug of beer after beer. He's in Kentucky. The leaves must be falling where he is, great mounds you'd have to kick through to the car. Leaves and loneliness. Leaves in our middle years.

What Carolyn was thinking I don't know. She smoked quietly, shuddering occasionally from the chilly evening wind, and faced the neighbor's house where a young couple lives. And they *are* young. When I stop them to say hello, they seem unable to talk without holding hands. They lean into each other, hip against hip, and wave a bashful hello, then are gone up the street.

Love birds, I chuckle to myself, they'll get over it. But maybe they won't. I hope not. Perhaps love will hold up enough mirrors so that tenderness will see them through life. It should be that way. Let them hold hands, and be happy.

Carolyn looked in the direction of their house. The shaded window was yellow. Now and then a blot of shadows filled the window as one of them walked past, readying for bed. For us the quiet of the yard should have been a first step toward sleep, but my mind was awake as it recalled how my own heart raced like a mouse in its cage, banging to get out, when I first met Carolyn. I was college poor, a boy with nothing more than books and an old car. But still she said yes. Still she let me lie with her on the couch and let me make foolish promises that my brother and roommates pretended not to hear, even though I heard them laugh and close the door and laugh harder. Finally it had come, love and its spinning craziness. I held her hand and glowed an initial happiness that won't ever come back. That was thirteen years ago. Six cities. Two countries. Roomful of friends. A daughter with her own life.

Much has come and gone, love and those days when it was not love. How do we add them up? Who are we supposed to be after so many years? I know nothing about this, except that in a small way we are different from when we first started off. A line inches across her brow; the flesh gathers under her chin; a thin fountain of white hair is beginning where there was once a shiny black. We wake up to mirrors, fix ourselves as best we can, and go our own way during the day and come back in the evening. I'm always happy to see my wife. Her soul is a blue flame in my heart, not the jagged teeth of love-flames that sent us down a church aisle to stand before a Japanese minister who said things I couldn't make out. I watched his face, pinched with a seriousness that fascinated me, and wondered what his blessings were all about.

Last week we sat in the dark. Music was two or three houses away. A screen door slammed and a burly voice said, "Kitty, kitty, kitty." There was a sound of cat food rattling from a box. I got up and snuggled up to Carolyn because I was cold and imagined that she too was cold from the wind that had picked up, though neither of us wanted to go inside. She shuddered when I placed a cold hand against her belly. I brushed back her hair. I kissed her neck, rubbed my hand against her arm for warmth and was nibbling my way down to her throat when I saw our cat Pip walking toward us from across the lawn. Sitting up, we both watched her approach and stop at our feet. "Pip," I said, "Pip, you ole' cat," petting her. I stopped my petting when I saw that her nose was twice its usual size. "What happened, baby?" I bent down to pick her up, but threw it away when I realized with a start that an *animal*, not our cat, was in my hands. I let out a clipped scream that was almost a laugh while Carolyn gripped my arm and asked, "What's wrong?" not certain what my fear was about. She bent down to take a closer look at Pip, and screamed, kicking her feet up onto the bench.

I laughed wildly and thought it strange that a possum (we had guessed from its slow crawl and spooky white fur like dirty pajamas) should show up in our yard. "Let's go inside, you first." I poked Carolyn to hurry up. She poked me back, hard, and said for me to be a man. We raced each other to the porch from where we looked back. We went inside and from our bedroom window listened to the possum clunk around in the yard and finally claw itself up the fence and disappear, leaving us still breathing hard but happy. We turned away from the window, undressed, and went to bed where we talked about our friend in Europe and pressed against each other. My hand, by then warn, asked her hip, "What do you want?" This, her hand said, and moved my arm across her shoulder. This for a long time.